MURDER MOST FOUL

I used my foot to slide the box partially off the body, enough to see the face belonging to the foot and leg. Looking up at me was the round, ruddy face of Daisy—I didn't know her last name—the young woman who had served us dinner the night before at Sutherland Castle.

My fist went to my mouth to stifle the anguished cry about to erupt. A pitchfork rose from Daisy's chest. The handle had been broken off just above the metal tines. Brown dried blood surrounded each tooth.

I crouched lower. I hadn't seen it at first glance. Carved into her throat was a small, bloody cross.

MURDER, SHE WROTE
THE HIGHLAND FLING
MURDERS

THE HIGHLAND FLING MURDERS

A *Murder, She Wrote* Mystery

A Novel by Jessica Fletcher

and Donald Bain

based on the

Universal television series

created by Peter S. Fischer,

Richard Levinson & William Link

A SIGNET BOOK

SIGNET
Published by New American Library, a division of
Penguin Group (USA) Inc., 375 Hudson Street,
New York, New York 10014, USA
Penguin Group (Canada), 90 Eglinton Avenue East, Suite 700, Toronto,
Ontario M4P 2Y3, Canada (a division of Pearson Penguin Canada Inc.)
Penguin Books Ltd., 80 Strand, London WC2R 0RL, England
Penguin Ireland, 25 St. Stephen's Green, Dublin 2,
Ireland (a division of Penguin Books Ltd.)
Penguin Group (Australia), 250 Camberwell Road, Camberwell, Victoria 3124,
Australia (a division of Pearson Australia Group Pty. Ltd.)
Penguin Books India Pvt. Ltd., 11 Community Centre, Panchsheel Park,
New Delhi - 110 017, India
Penguin Group (NZ), 67 Apollo Drive, Rosedale, North Shore 0632,
New Zealand (a division of Pearson New Zealand Ltd.)
Penguin Books (South Africa) (Pty.) Ltd., 24 Sturdee Avenue,
Rosebank, Johannesburg 2196, South Africa

Penguin Books Ltd., Registered Offices:
80 Strand, London WC2R 0RL, England

First published by Signet, an imprint of New American Library,
a division of Penguin Group (USA) Inc.

First Printing, April 1997
20   19   18

Copyright © 1997 Universal City Studios Productions LLLP. *Murder, She Wrote*
is a trademark and copyright of Universal Studios. All rights reserved.

Ⓤ REGISTERED TRADEMARK — MARCA REGISTRADA

Printed in the United States of America

For Laurie, Pamela, Billy, Marisa,
Alexander, Zachary, and Jacob.

Ah, youth!

And for my father, George Sutherland Bain,
who left Scotland to seek a better life
in America when the herring stopped running
in Wick, and who taught me
"Set a stoot hert to a stey brae."

"The harder the task,
the more determination is needed."

Chapter One

"Before Candlemas we went by East Kinloss, and then we yoked a plewghe of paddokis (frogs or toads). The divill held the plewghe, and John Younge in Mebestone, our officer, did drwe the plewghe. Paddokis did draw the plewghe as oxen, quickens (twitch-grass) were somes (traces), a ram's horn was a cowter; and a piece of ram's horn was a sok (yoke). We went two several times about; and all we of the covin went still up and down with the plewghe praying to the divill for the fruit of that land, and that thistles and briers might grow there."

"I thought they spoke English there, Mrs. F.," Cabot Cove's sheriff, and my good friend, Mort Metzger, said after reading what I'd handed him.

I laughed. "They do, Mort. But this was the way they spoke in sixteen twenty-two."

Mort had just read part of a confession made in 1622 by Scotland's most celebrated witch, Isabell

Gowdie. It was, she'd told her accusers, a special curse often used by her coven. George Sutherland, my Scottish friend and a chief inspector with Scotland Yard in London, had included it in a long letter to me, which I shared with my friends at Boston's Logan Airport while waiting to board our British Airways flight to London.

"Gives me the chills," said Alicia Richardson as she read George Sutherland's description in his letter of how Isabell Gowdie had died—a pitchfork through her chest, pinning her to the ground, her throat slashed with two strokes of a knife, creating a cross. According to George, a descendant of Isabell had settled in his hometown, Wick, Scotland, and had died in the same manner only twenty years ago.

"Lot of nonsense," Sheriff Metzger muttered. "Sounds like your friend Sutherland is a mite *queeuh*."

Alicia's husband, Jed Richardson—Alicia was his third wife; she was twenty-six, Jed forty-seven—a former airline pilot, was now owner, operator, and only pilot for Jed's Flying Service, operating out of Cabot Cove's tiny single-strip airport. He said of his pretty, bubbly redheaded wife, "Alicia won't sleep a wink while we're there. She believes in ghosts."

"I do not," she said, waving his comment away with her hand. "Still—"

There were twelve of us from Cabot Cove about to embark on a trip to Great Britain.

Our plans to travel together had coalesced quickly. It started when my British publisher, Archibald Semple, persuaded me to come to England to promote my latest mystery novel there. His edition had just come out, and he felt it needed the sort of boost only the author can provide by appearing on radio and television, and giving interviews to print media. I agreed, of course, and called a friend, Susan Shevlin, owner of Cabot Cove's best travel agency.

After planning and booking my trip, Susan suggested that she and her husband, Jim, who'd recently been elected mayor of Cabot Cove, accompany me to London. That started the ball rolling. Soon, through Susan's efforts, nine others had signed on: Morton and Maureen Metzger; Dr. Seth Hazlitt; the Richardsons; Peter and Roberta Walters, owners of Cabot Cove's small and only radio station; Charlene Sassi of Sassi's Bakery and Restaurant, and husband, Ken, the area's best fishing guide; and, of course, Susan and Jim Shevlin.

But then the plot thickened, as they say.

When I told George Sutherland I was coming to England, he insisted I extend my trip to spend time at his family's castle in Wick, Scotland, on the northernmost coast.

"I really can't, George," I replied. "I'm traveling with other people. Eleven of them."

"Not a problem, Jessica," he said. "The old family homestead has fourteen rooms. Since I seldom have a chance to get there, and because it costs a bloody fortune to maintain, it's rented out as a hotel most of the year. There's a staff, a fine kitchen and chef, the works. Bookings have been slow. There are only two couples booked in for the time you and your friends would be there. Please. You know I've been trying to entice you to Wick ever since we met. Say yes."

"Yes," I said. "I'll check with the others and let you know how many can extend their trip."

As it turned out, everyone decided to venture north with me to George's castle on the tail end of my book-promotion tour.

The announcement that came through the lounge's speakers sent a tingle of pleasure through me, as it always does. I'm an unabashed Anglophile, and that includes British Airways and its unrivaled service to London: *"British Airways flight two-oh-seven, service to London, is now boarding at gate number four."*

"That's us," Seth Hazlitt said, slinging his carry-on bag over his shoulder.

We made our way to the gate, checked through, and settled in our seats in the spacious 747 aircraft. Had I been traveling alone, I would have been booked in first, or business class, compliments of the publisher. But with my friends seated in the back, it would have been insensitive, to say nothing of depriving me of the fun of being with them on a long flight. Spirits were high, conversation sprightly, and the trip went by quickly.

We landed precisely on time at Heathrow Airport, and passed through Customs. A long line of those wonderful, civilized black London taxis stood waiting just outside the luggage area. We picked up our luggage and put them on free trolleys available to arriving passengers. It took three cabs to accommodate us, each driven by polite, intelligent drivers who put cabbies everywhere else in the world to shame.

"You say this Athenaeum Hotel is a classy place?" Ken Sassi, the fishing guide, asked.

"Oh, yes," I said. "I stayed there the last time I was in London."

"Thought you were partial to the Dorchester," Charlene Sassi said.

"I was. I am. I love it. But the Athenaeum has a special—a special *feeling* to it. You'll love it. Trust me."

The twelve of us had no sooner stepped into the small, stylish lobby off Piccadilly, when Sally Bulloch burst from the elevator, saw me, closed the gap between us in a flash, and gave me a big hug. "I've been waiting for you," she said. "Good flight? They feed you good? My goodness, Jessica, you look splendid. A new book in the works? I picked up your latest. You'll sign it, of course. These must be your friends—"

I burst out laughing. Sally Bulloch was so brimming over with energy and spirit that it tumbled out of her every waking minute. No wonder she'd become such a legend in London that the Athenaeum's restaurant was named after her.

"Everyone," I said, "this is Sally Bulloch, the executive manager."

"Welcome," she said, pretty face beaming. "Come on. The bar is open." With that, she was on her way across the lobby in the direction of the Athenaeum's famed watering hole, the Malt Whisky Bar, where seventy single-malt whiskeys are featured.

"Sally," I said.

She stopped, turned, and cocked her head.

"I think we all need to get to our rooms first. Rain check?"

She laughed. "Absolutely."

A few minutes later we were led to our rooms by nattily dressed young bellhops. The moment mine had departed, I kicked off my shoes, opened the drapes, and looked out over London. What a splendid city, I thought, one of my favorite places on this earth.

I unpacked, and was in the process of hanging

my clothes in the closet when the phone rang. I picked up the closest of three in the suite. "Jessica Fletcher," I said.

"Jessica. Archie Semple here."

"Hello, Archie. How are you?"

"Splendid, now that you've arrived. I realized how negligent I'd been in not arranging transportation for you from the airport."

"I'm glad you didn't. I'm traveling with eleven good friends. I think I mentioned that to you last time we talked."

"That's right. You did. Bloody big group to have in tow."

"Yes it is. But they understand I can't spend much time with them while I'm promoting my book. Speaking of that, when do I start?"

"This evening. At dinner. An interview with the *Times*'s leading book critic. Delightful lady. Margaret Swales. You can call her Maggie."

"Off to a running start, I see. Where and when?"

"I'll swing by the Athenaeum at seven. Busy day tomorrow, too. Still planning to venture north to the land of the barbarians?"

" 'Land of the barbarians'? You mean Scotland?"

He let out with a hearty laugh, punctuated by a loud cough. He obviously still smoked his dreaded cigars.

"Why do you call Scotland barbaric?" I asked.

"Because of their bloody violent history. Bloody. The proper word. Grown men running around in skirts. Bloody bizarre, I say. Bloody foolish."

I wasn't in the mood to debate it, so simply said I'd be ready by seven.

The Cabot Cove contingent had agreed to meet in the Malt Whisky Bar in an hour. I showered and dressed for the evening before going downstairs to join them. I was the last arrival. By the time I got there, my friends were into serious tasting of the bar's large single-malt scotch inventory.

"Look here, Mrs. F.," Mort Metzger said, handing me a menu. "After you drink each scotch, you check it off on this list. Taste all seventy of 'em, they give you a free bottle."

"You aren't intending to do that, are you?"

"Not me. But maybe they'd let us do it as a group."

"I don't think that's the purpose," I said.

"Hi."

Sally Bulloch pranced into the bar area, her blond hair bouncing in rhythm with her step. "Everything peachy?"

"Yes." It was a chorus.

"Say, Ms. Bulloch, could I have a word with you?" Mort Metzger asked.

"In a minute," she replied, moving to other tables; she seemed to know everyone in the room.

"Are you going to ask her whether our group can taste all the scotches?" I asked Mort.

"Thought I would."

"Don't. It puts her in an awkward position."

"*Ayuh*," Seth Hazlitt chimed in. "Damn foolish idea anyway."

"They're giving a free bottle," Mort said.

"And that's not a reason to—"

Sally reappeared, ending the conversation between Mort and Seth. "You wanted to ask me something," she said to Mort.

Mort glanced at me and Seth before saying, "Just wondered whether you could recommend a good restaurant for us. I know British food isn't much, but—"

"British food is very good now, Mort," I said.

Sally laughed. "It is in *my* restaurant. Why don't you eat here? We're featuring breast of Barbary duck with bubble and squeak tonight."

" 'Bubble and squeak'?" Charlene Sassi, the group's most knowledgeable cook, asked.

"A little cabbage, a little potato. You'll love it."

"Got anything simpler?" Mort asked.

"Chicken simple enough?"

"I figure," he said.

"Are you eating with us, Jess?" radio station owner Peter Walters asked.

15

"Afraid not. I'm being interviewed by someone from the *London Times*."

"We'll miss you," Walters's wife, Roberta, said.

"Why don't we all meet back here after dinner," Seth suggested.

"Fine idea," I said. "I can't promise, but I'll try. Have to run and do a few things before I'm picked up. Have dinner here. The chef is wonderful. My favorite's the charbroiled sea bass. See you later."

Chapter Two

My British publisher, Archibald Semple, is a dear man with a bevy of bad personal traits. He's quite obese, and defines slovenliness, tending to perspire in even the coolest of settings. His suits, expensive no doubt, look horribly cheap on him because of his corpulent frame, and he has a penchant for what the British often call "dickey bows," large, floppy bow ties. His fingernails are always highly lacquered, something I find unattractive in men, and he attempts to cover a broad expanse of bald head by bringing up long, wet strands of hair from just above his left ear.

But it's when dining with Archie Semple that one is called upon to keep a stiff upper lip. He consumes food with the zeal of a starving pack of wolves, much of it ending up on an assortment of ties that are, to be kind, dreadful.

Other than that, I love him dearly. He's an astute and effective publisher, one who has taken each of my novels and turned them into best-sellers in Great Britain.

He picked me up in a limousine driven by a handsome young man in uniform. After preliminary and perfunctory greetings, we headed for Wilton's on Jermyn Street, one of London's finest restaurants. I'd had dinner there the last time I visited London; its chef has elevated what used to be pedestrian English food to fine cuisine.

Margaret Swales was a birdlike older woman with an infectious laugh. She wore a garish purple dress adorned with heavy strands of jewelry, and a small purple pillbox hat from a bygone era. What was especially charming about her was her intense interest in my responses to her questions. She had many of them.

Over a sumptuous meal beginning with oyster cocktails, proceeding to plain Dover sole for me, roast wigeon—a wild, fish-eating river duck served only when in season—for Archibald and Ms. Swales, and topped off with sherry trifle, the conversation gradually shifted to a discussion of British mystery writers, and crimes real and imagined.

"... Of course, we Brits tend to call mysteries 'thrillers,' even when they aren't thrilling at all," Maggie said, sipping tea. "We're accused of being claustrophobic in our approach to the mystery, although I must say I'm rather comfortable being cloistered in a room with a villain about to commit deadly mischief on someone else."

I laughed. "I love cozy mysteries, too," I said, "but have trouble plotting them. Your British writers seem to have a special knack for it."

"I suppose. But I've lately developed an appetite for true crime, especially those with historical significance."

Archie Semple chimed in: "We're beefing up our true-crime list at Semple House. I quite agree with you. Truth, indeed, can be stranger than fiction. We've signed up a marvelous young chap to do a book on the Lydia Duncomb murder. A real sizzler."

"I'm not familiar with that," I said.

"Seventeen thirty-two, Tanfield Court, the Temple. No reason you should know of it, Jessica, being a Yank and all."

"I haven't been called that in years," I said.

"Brutal murder," said Margaret Swales. "Strangled in her flat. Her maid's throat slit, too. The murderess, Sarah Malcolm, was escorted to the gallows at Temple Gate by a man of the cloth who'd fallen in love with her."

Archie rubbed his hands together. "Bloody juicy stuff, wouldn't you say, Jessica? The only surprise is that it didn't take place in bloody Scotland."

Margaret Swales laughed at the comment. "Yes, the Scots have had their share of gruesome murders, particularly up north, the Highlands, on the coast.''

Archie looked at me for a comment. I didn't have one. We ended dinner on the pleasant note of Ms. Swales pledging to do a lengthy article on me and my new book, which delighted Archie.

As we were leaving Wilton's, Archie stopped to say hello to a man at another table, who was with three other people. ''Marshall,'' he said, ''meet Jessica.''

The man, who was short and slender and expensively dressed, stood and shook my hand. ''*The* Jessica Fletcher?'' he said.

''Afraid so,'' I said.

''A real pleasure. Archie's star author.''

''I hope not,'' I said.

''We'll wrap things up tomorrow?'' Archie asked.

''Absolutely. The solicitors will be there. Shouldn't be a hitch.''

''Good. See you then, Marshall.''

Back in the limo, Archie asked whether I wanted to go to his club for a nightcap and further ''chat.''

''Love to, Archie, but I promised my friends I'd meet them at the hotel. They're quite content not seeing me very much, but I would like to spend as much time together as possible.''

''I can certainly understand that, Jessica. The fellow I introduced you to. Marshall Flemming. Flemming Publishing. Heard of them?"

"Can't say that I have."

"Very successful. Subsidy publishers. Pay them, they publish your book."

"We have a number of those in the States."

"Yes you do. Keep a secret?"

"I'll do my best."

"I'm about to buy Flemming Publishing. Should wrap up the deal in the morning. Bloody successful group. Offices in London, Birmingham, Edinburgh, and Glasgow."

"Congratulations. Will it remain a subsidy publisher?"

"Absolutely. Not that I'm about to have Semple House publish subsidized works. I'll keep it a separate division."

"Why would you buy it if you don't want to get into subsidized publishing?" I asked.

"Cash flow, my dear. My profit margins are being dreadfully squeezed these days. The entire publishing industry is feeling it. Having Flemming House's strong cash flow will make all the difference, give me the financial wherewithal to go after bigger and better mainstream books."

"Sounds like a prudent business decision," I said.

"I think it will be. Well, let's get you back safely to the Athenaeum. How's Sally Bulloch?"

"As bouncy as ever. If I were to give her a nickname, it would be Buoyant Bulloch."

He laughed. "Quite good, Jessica. She ought to write a book. Lord knows, she's as much a fixture in London as—well, perhaps not as much of a fixture as Big Ben and the Tower, but close."

I didn't disagree.

We parted in front of the hotel with Archie handing me my itinerary for the following day. It was a busy one; getting a good night's sleep was very much in order.

The Athenaeum's lobby was bustling with well-dressed people. I made my way through them and entered the Malt Whisky Bar, which was even more crowded. Cigar and cigarette smoke created a heavy blue cloud over the heads of customers. I spotted my group in a far corner.

"Jessica, I was wondering whether you'd get here," Jim Shevlin said, standing and offering me his chair.

"I made it," I said. "But I'm not staying long. My publisher has set up a brutal schedule for me tomorrow, and my circadian rhythms are annoyingly out of kilter. But I will taste a single-malt scotch, just because I think I should."

To my amazement, Sally Bulloch was still going strong, flitting from one group to another, making sure they were happy and comfortable, exchanging quips, laughing and joking with her hotel's guests, as she would do in her own home. That's what I enjoy about the Athenaeum. It's like being home in a room filled with friends.

It wasn't until I'd ordered a scotch called Laphroaig, and winced at its intense peaty flavor, that I realized that Alicia Richardson and her husband, Jed, weren't there. I asked about them.

"They took off on their own, Mrs. F.," Mort Metzger said. "We ate here. Great food. But Jed and Alicia said they weren't hungry and felt like taking a long walk. You know Jed. Like Ken, here. Never can sit still. All they talked about on the flight was fishing for trout and salmon. They sure love the outdoors."

"I hope they know where they're going," I said to no one in particular.

I stayed with the group for a half hour before yawning, standing, and wishing them all pleasant dreams. It was as I started to drift off in my comfortable king-size bed that I thought of Jed and Alicia. They hadn't returned by the time I left the bar, and I began to worry about them. London is a safe city by world standards. But still—

Blessed sleep displaced any further worries about them.

Chapter Three

My phone rang at six the next morning. It was Seth Hazlitt. "Jessica," he said, "we've got a problem."

I sat up and rubbed my eyes. "A problem? What sort of problem?"

"Jed and Alicia never came back."

I was wide awake.

"Ken checked in on them. You know Ken and Jed, always up before the sun. Nobody in their room. Ken checked the desk. Their room key's still there. Never picked up."

"Do you think—?"

"I don't know what to think, Jessica, 'cept there's got to be a reason for it, probably not a pleasant one."

"Do the others know?"

"Nope. Thought I'd talk to you first before gettin' them all riled up. Occurred to me your friend, Sutherland, might be a help in this."

"Of course. He was out of town yesterday attending a conference in Birmingham. Came back to London last night, I believe. I'll try him at home."

"Meet me in the lobby in a half hour?"

"I'll be there."

Scotland Yard Chief Inspector George Sutherland answered on the first ring. "Jessica, so good to hear your voice."

"Did I wake you?"

"No. I have an early meeting at the Yard. Always seems to be a meeting to attend these days, most a waste of time. How was your trip?"

"Fine. I—"

"I can't wait to have you and your friends visit in Wick. I'll be going up a day ahead to—"

"George, can we discuss this a little later? I have a problem I thought you might help with."

"Anything."

I explained the situation.

"I'll have an all points put out on them immediately. Give me their names and descriptions."

After I had, he asked, "Any hint of where they might have gone last night? A destination? A direction? Do they have friends here? Relatives?"

"Not that I'm aware of, George. I'm meeting one of my friends downstairs in a half hour."

"I'll be there."

"What about your meeting?"

"This is a police emergency. See you in a half hour."

Seth was pacing the lobby when I arrived. Ken and Charlene Sassi sipped coffee in a corner. I'd no sooner greeted them when George Sutherland strode through the door. He was as handsome as ever, six feet, four inches tall (no need to guess at his age any longer; I knew he was sixty-one), brown hair tinged with a hint of red, distinguished accents of gray at the temples. His eyes were the color of Granny Smith apples. This day he wore a tan trench coat over a blue suit, white shirt and muted red-and-blue-striped tie. His smile was wide and warm as he came directly to me and extended his large hand, which I took. He kissed me on the cheek and said, "It's been too long since last laying eyes on you, Jess."

I was aware that Seth and the Sassis were observing us, so I turned to them and said, "This is Scotland Yard Chief Inspector George Sutherland."

Ken and Charlene shook his hand. George extended it to Seth Hazlitt. They'd met previously during one of my London trips, the one, in fact, that resulted in my meeting George. Seth had always expressed a certain reservation about George, probably because I'd demonstrated positive personal feelings for my Scottish friend on a few occasions. They shook hands.

"Now," said George, "tell me about this missing couple."

Ken Sassi told him about unsuccessfully trying to contact the Richardsons in their room, and that their key hadn't been picked up last night.

"I've put out an all points bulletin on your friends," George said. "Local police are looking for them as we speak. I suggest we gather together the rest of your party. Someone might have an idea as to where they've gone, what they intended to do last night."

Soon, all ten of us, plus George, were in the lobby. Seth filled in the latecomers on why we were there, his announcement eliciting a variety of responses and comments. Mort Metzger, sheriff of Cabot Cove, who'd met George Sutherland in London at the same time Seth had, slipped from being a tourist back into his law-enforcement mode, sans uniform. He started issuing orders, and loudly questioned whether the London police and Scotland Yard were doing enough to find Jed and Alicia. George listened patiently, a thin smile on his lips. He'd heard this before from Mort when we were all together in London.

When Mort was finished, George said, "Every bobby in the city is searching for your friends. The Yard's missing person bureau has also joined the search. I'm going back to headquarters to coordinate the effort." To me: "Jess, I'll keep in touch through you."

"That will be difficult, George. I have a series of interviews all over the city."

"No problem," Mort said, up on his toes, chest puffed. "I'll work with you, Inspector. We can talk lawman to lawman."

"If you insist," said George. He winked at me and left.

Mort addressed us. "I'll stay here at the hotel command post. I suggest you work in pairs. We'll divvy up directions and head out. North, south, east, and west. Somebody got a map?"

"I do," Ken Sassi said, pulling one from his British Airways shoulder bag and handing it to our sheriff.

"Which way is the Tower of London?" Pete Walters asked. Pete has a deep baritone voice, which he puts to good use in radio. He does a daily show on the tiny AM station he and his wife own in Cabot Cove, broadcasting only from sunrise to sunset but keeping the community informed of its daily comings and goings, a weekly newspaper of the air.

Mort looked up from the map. "Why do you ask that, Pete?"

"Because that's where they were going last night," Pete replied.

"Why didn't you say so before?" Susan Shevlin asked.

"Nobody asked until just a few minutes ago. Roberta and I didn't even know Jed and Alicia were missing until now."

"How do you know they were going to the Tower of London?" someone asked.

"They showed us the tickets on the flight," Roberta Walters said. "They wrote weeks ago for them. Alicia told me the guidebook she bought for the trip said that if she and Jed wanted to attend an evening ceremony at the London Tower—what's it called, Peter? Ceremony of the Keys? Something like that.

"Ceremony of the Keys," Roberta repeated. "If they wanted to attend it, they had to write at least six weeks in advance. So Alicia wrote."

"The Tower of London," Mort mumbled. "That's where all those folks got killed. I read about it."

"I suggest we get going," I said. "The Tower is obviously the place to start looking."

We were about to move out when Sally Bulloch stepped from the elevators. "What's up?" she asked. "Early for sightseeing, isn't it?"

I was about to explain when she said, "Too many kooks in this world, Jessica."

"What do you mean?"

"You didn't hear? There's a demented bloke

holding two people hostage at the Tower of London."

"Two people?" Jim Shevlin said.

"Right you are," answered Sally. "A man and a woman."

"We're missing two people," I said. "A man and a woman." I quickly explained our situation.

"Sally," one of two desk clerks said, "there's a call for a Sheriff Metzger."

Mort took the phone. "That so?" he said. "Looks like it. Just heard about it ourselves. Okay."

"Was that George Sutherland?" I asked when he rejoined us.

"*Ayuh.* Called from his car. Looks like it could be Jed and Alicia this nut's got at the Tower."

"What else did George say?"

"Says the guy wants to speak before Congress here."

"The Parliament, you mean," Sally said.

"Whatever. Says he's a descendant of some British woman who was burned at the stake. Here. I wrote down her name." He handed a slip of paper to me. *Catherine Hayes. 1725.* "He says this nut wants to talk to Congress—"

"Parliament," Sally corrected.

"Parliament. Says he wants to clear this Hayes lady's name. Claims he'll kill his hostages unless he gets to do it."

"Did George say he was heading for the Tower?" I asked.

"*Ayuh*. Reckon we should do the same."

We piled into three taxis parked in front of the Athenaeum and headed for London's famed Tower of London, also known as "the Bloody Tower" because of its nine hundred years of brutal history.

Being locked up there in Tudor times was synonymous with death—Anne Boleyn, Catherine Howard, Lady Jane Grey, Sir Thomas More, and Sir Walter Raleigh are just a few who spent their final days in the forbidding Tower and adjacent buildings. I'd learned a lot about it when researching a talk I once gave to the Mystery Writers of America. Many say that London's first notorious murder occurred at the Tower when two little princes were suffocated on the orders of their uncle, Richard III, in the fifteenth century, in order to secure the throne for himself. Their tiny bones weren't found until the seventeenth century, buried beneath a staircase.

Sir Walter Raleigh made good use of his time in the Tower. He was there from 1603 until 1616, and wrote his impressive *A History of the World* while a prisoner.

Today, the Tower of London is anything but a brutal prison. The famed Crown Jewels are housed there; fifty families reside within its walls, and use the 120-foot-wide moat, now covered with green grass, for picnics. Still, each time I've visited, I've had this pervasive feeling of doom, and torture, and death by decapitation. I ended my talk to the mystery writers by quoting from James Street: "There are more spooks to the square foot than in any other building in the whole of haunted Britain. Headless bodies, bodiless heads, phantom soldiers, icy blasts, clanking chains—you name them, the Tower's got them."

All silly, of course.

Except that now two dear friends were being held there by a demented man who threatens to kill them unless he is granted his absurd request.

I quickly perused one of my guidebooks that had a section on London murders of yesteryear. Sure enough, there was a paragraph describing how one Catherine Hayes murdered and dismembered her husband in 1725, scattering his body parts all over London. According to the book, she was the last person to be burned at the stake in London for "petty treason"—murdering her husband.

By the time we'd crossed the city—past Trafalgar and down the Strand to St. Paul's Cathedral—the scene at the Tower was chaos. Dozens of official vehicles clogged the streets. The police were everywhere. Areas had been roped off, keeping hundreds of onlookers at bay. We were kept from crossing the police lines until I spotted George Sutherland, who came directly to us.

"Is it them?" I asked.

"Don't have their names, Jess. The woman is a redhead and pretty. Fellow is husky, sort of blond hair. Leathery face."

"Jed and Alicia," I muttered. "How bad is it?"

"The man continues to demand time before Parliament. He says that if he doesn't get it, your two friends will join others who've lost their lives in the Tower. Intelligent chap, it seems. Spouts history when we talk to him. Seems to know a lot. But then he starts babbling about this long-lost relative, and the need to clear her name and reputation."

"I take it he's armed," I said.

"We've seen two handguns."

"Are you handling the hostage negotiations?"

"By default."

"Can we come with you, see firsthand what's happening?"

"Afraid not. Well, you can, Jess. But just one person."

"Hold on a second," Mort Metzger said. "As a law enforcement official of Cabot Cove, Maine, U.S.A., I am responsible for the safety of our citizens. That goes here, too. I'm comin' in with you."

George looked at me with eyes that pleaded for

me to say something to Mort. But then he said, "All right, Sheriff. You and Jessica."

We made our way through the throng until we'd reached where George conducted his negotiations with the abductor. I was surprised at how close we were to him, no more than thirty feet. A shield had been put in place, behind which George used a powered bullhorn to talk with the kidnapper. My friends could be seen through a small window. They appeared to be kneeling, the hostage-taker standing right behind them. Alicia saw me and yelled, "Jess! Go back."

I waved away her plea and joined Mort behind the shield. We crouched low, next to George, who picked up the bullhorn and said, "It should be evident to you, sir, that you are surrounded. Killing these innocent Americans will accomplish nothing except a life in prison. If you release them now and come out peacefully, I'm sure the right people will listen to your grievances about your relative, Ms. Hayes; perhaps even allow certain members of Parliament to hear you out. But if you harm them, there can be no discussion. You will be killed."

"I thought you fellas didn't use guns," Mort said.

"Not in public," George said, his eyes trained on the window. "But if the situation warrants—"

"The government ruined my family name in

seventeen twenty-five and continues to do it," the abductor shouted. "I'll let these filthy rich Americans go if you promise me an hour before the bloody bastards of Parliament."

"George, can I respond?" I asked.

"What? You?"

"Yes. Please."

"Have a go, Jess."

He handed me the bullhorn. I tentatively put it to my lips, cleared my throat, and said, "Sir, my name is Jessica Fletcher. I write murder mysteries."

I looked over the shield. Jed and Alicia's captor had a confused expression on his face. Jed had slightly shifted position; his rugged, handsome face, so heavily lined from thousands of hours peering into the sun through aircraft windshields, was clearly visible to me. I only hoped he wouldn't try to disarm the madman himself. Jed was a strong, rugged man, but no match for two weapons.

"The two people you're holding are very good friends of mine. They've done nothing to hurt you. If you have a gripe with your government, this is not the way to air it."

The man said nothing. I stood to my full height.

"Get down, Mrs. F.," Mort Metzger said, grabbing my arm.

I pulled away from his grasp, stepped around the shield, and started toward the window.

"Jessica," George said, reaching for me.

I continued walking, my hands outstretched in a gesture of peace.

"*Jessica!*" George shouted.

I kept walking. When I was only a few feet from the window, I said, "Young man, if you insist upon holding an American hostage, you can hold me. I'm a writer. *I'll* listen to your story. Let them go!"

I wondered if he saw my trembling legs and heaving chest.

"No, Jess, stay away," Jed Richardson said.

"Let them go," I said. "I'll see to it that you have a chance to vent your anger and concerns. Don't be foolish. If you don't let them go, you'll—"

I froze as he stepped back, and Jed and Alicia stood. A moment later, a door opened and my friends stepped through it. They started toward me, but I told them to get behind the shield.

I didn't know what to do next. The demented man looked as though he expected me to come through the door and join him in his cramped hideout. I wasn't about to do that, of course. But I was afraid that once I started back to safety, he might shoot.

There was no choice.

I slowly, deliberately turned and took a step in the direction of George, Mort, and the protective shield. I listened for the ominous metallic sound of a hammer being cocked—or worse—of a gun going off.

I took another step. And another. I wanted desperately to run to safety, but kept my fears in check. To bolt might prompt him to involuntarily fire.

I saw the grave expressions on Mort, George, Jed, and Alicia's faces, eyes wide, lips compressed into thin, anxious lines.

When I reached the shield, George grabbed my arm and yanked me behind it. As he did, the sound of a weapon firing cut through the foggy morning, its bullet striking the shield and ricocheting to the ground.

I lost it at that point. My legs, now jelly, failed to support me, and I sank to my knees, wrapping my arms around myself and leaning forward, trembling, muttering words that meant nothing. A cacophony of sounds erupted around me as police units rushed the abductor and subdued him. He didn't fire another shot.

The press now converged as George led Mort, the Richardsons, and me to the street. A wedge of uniformed London officers kept the reporters and cameras at bay until we reached the rest of my

Cabot Cove traveling companions. They all verbally assaulted me at once.

George came to my rescue: "Jess has been through a traumatic experience. I suggest we get her back to the hotel and let her rest."

Jed and Alicia went to police headquarters to give a statement. Mort and the others took cabs back to the Athenaeum. George drove me in his unmarked car.

"I just remembered I have interviews to get to," I said as he turned on to Piccadilly.

"Cancel them, Jess. You don't realize what you've been through. It will hit you later, like a truck."

"No," I said. "I'll be all right." I checked my watch. "I have just enough time to shower and change before my first interview."

"Won't change your mind?"

"No. Thank you, George."

He laughed. "For what? *You* saved the day for your friends."

"For being here. For being—you."

He stopped in front of the hotel. "Not a very nice way to begin your visit, Jess."

"Oh, just a little excitement. I have to get inside, George. You say you're going up to Wick a day or two ahead of us. Will I see you again in London before that?"

"Absolutely. Jess, I have to ask you a question."

"Go ahead."

"Why did you do what you did this morning?
Approach that madman."

I opened the door, stepped out of the car, and
closed the door behind me. I leaned in through
the open window and said, "George, I have absolutely no idea why I did it. If I'd thought about
it, I never would have. And now that I *am* thinking about it, I'm scared to death. I'll be in touch."

I blew him a kiss and ran into the lobby.

Chapter Four

George had been right. The impact of my morning at the Tower of London hit me at eleven o'clock, right in the middle of an interview with the BBC. I managed to hide the pain and fatigue I felt, but once I walked from the studio and out onto the street, accompanied by Archie Semple's director of publicity, I felt so faint I had to lean against a building

"Feeling sick, Mrs. Fletcher?" the publicist asked.

"Yes. It's been a—an interesting morning." I stood straight, took a few deep breaths, and smiled. "What's next?"

The rest of the London portion of the trip went smoothly, complicated only by press interest in my experience in helping free Jed and Alicia Richardson. Some government officials wanted to fete me at a banquet, but I managed to slip out of those commitments, falling back on the fact that

I'd be returning to London after our sojourn in Scotland. "Perhaps then," I said.

The most nettlesome aspect of the media interest was created by London's fabled tabloids. They'd decided that because Scotland Yard Chief Inspector George Sutherland and I would be spending time together at his family home in Wick, there must be something risqué to report. That I would be there with eleven chaperones from Cabot Cove didn't seem to matter. I tried to be gracious in deflecting their inquiries, but my annoyance came through too often.

Archie Semple was delighted with the media attention.

"The book is selling out in every bookstore, Jessica," he told me. "We've gone back to press for another thirty thousand. Best-seller list this coming Sunday in the *Times, Guardian,* and *Independent.* The *London Review of Books* is calling it your crossover book, Jessica, mainstream literature. The *London Observer* loves it. Absolutely l-o-v-e-s it! Tabloids are playing up your heroism big, full-page photos in the *Star* and *Sun.* Couldn't go better if we'd planned it."

I was pleased for Archie and his publishing house, of course. But as the week wore on, all I could think of was getting out of London and going to Scotland, where, I assumed, the pressure would be off and relaxation would be the order of the day. I pictured windswept cliffs and sparkling water, charming pubs and streams teeming with fat salmon. Ken Sassi had brought with him enough fly-fishing equipment for the two of us, and we promised each other a day on a stream, our artificial flies bobbing in clear, clean water, birds singing in the trees, and if we were lucky, the excitement of a sharp tug on the line and the sight of a salmon arching from the water, diving under again and playing out the line until I skillfully brought him to me where I would offer my verbal apologies, gently slip the barbless hook from his mouth, move him beneath the water a few times to force air through his gills, and send him off, hopefully having helped him gain a little more wisdom about telling the difference between real bugs and the hand-tied variety.

I love fly-fishing, and do it as often as time allows back home. It's the most liberating personal experience I know. The world disappears, all tension dissipates; there is only you and the water and the fish. I couldn't wait to sample the streams of Scotland, the most renowned in the world. And with Ken Sassi acting as my guide, as he'd done many times in Maine, I just knew I'd catch some fish, which didn't always happen back home. But then again, catching fish is not the most important thing for a fly fisherman, or woman. It's the *process* of fishing that counts. That's the goal, not the catching of anything except fresh breezes on your face and the feel of cold water through your waders.

The rest of the Cabot Cove party had a wonderful time in London that week, playing tourist, seeing the city's fabled sights, and soaking in its civilized splendor.

Sally Bulloch hosted a departure lunch for us in the restaurant named for her. A sleek bus waited outside to take us to Heathrow Airport for a flight to Inverness, near the home of the mythical Loch Ness Monster, where we would board a touring bus reserved exclusively for us for the rest of the trip north, to Wick, Scotland, "land of the barbarians" according to Archie Semple.

I'd mentioned Archie's comment to George Sutherland the day before he left for Wick to make sure things were ready for us. He replied, with a laugh, "Familiar with Finley Peter Dunne's *Mr. Dooley Remembers*, Jess?"

"Vaguely."

" 'The well-bred Englishman is about as agreeable a fellow as you can find anywhere—especially, as I have noted, if he is an Irishman or a Scotchman.' "

I laughed, too, but said, "I thought the proper term was 'Scotsman.' "

"Dunne had his weaknesses. It *is* Scotsman."

"I just thought of a line from George Bernard Shaw," I said.

"Which is?"

" 'Englishman—a creature who thinks he is being virtuous when he is only being uncomfortable.' "

"I'd forgotten that one. Well, this barbarian must be off. See you in Wick in a few days. Safe trip. And no more heroics, dear lady."

"You needn't worry about that, George." We pressed our cheeks to one another, and hugged, and I watched him get into a Scotland Yard car that would take him to the airport. I gave a final wave and headed for yet another interview.

"See you in a week or so," Sally Bulloch said as we got into the bus in front of the Athenaeum. She'd become like a friend of many years to everyone.

"Save our rooms," Jed Richardson said.

"Thanks for your hospitality, Sally," said Jim Shevlin.

"Bloody fine city you have here," Mort Metzger shouted, slapping his wide-brimmed Stetson on his thigh.

We were off on our Highland fling.

Spirits remained high on the way to the airport, and during the wait for our flight to be announced. The only exception was Alicia Richardson.

Since her terrifying ordeal at the Tower of London, she'd become quiet and restrained, unable or unwilling to participate in the group's merrymaking and laughter. I asked her about it as we sipped tea in the airport lounge.

"I don't know, Jess," she said. "Sure, it was scary and upsetting. But it's been a week since then, and I still—"

"You still what, Alicia?"

"I still feel his eyes on me. Did you see his eyes, Jess?"

"I don't remember them."

"They were like burning coals. They were orange."

"Orange?"

"Yes. Maybe not literally, but they had that tint. Mad eyes. Crazy eyes. Do you know what he told Jed and me?"

"That he would kill you if he didn't have his forum."

"After that. He said he would put a curse on us so that we would rot in Hell. A curse!"

My laugh was small and forced. "There's no such thing as a curse, Alicia." I lightly touched her arm. "At least none that work."

She shuddered and slumped in the chair.

"Alicia. Forget about any threat of a curse from a seriously demented man. The trip is such fun, and we'll all have a marvelous time in Wick. Don't let this madman's idle, stupid threat of a curse ruin your vacation."

"I'll try not to, Jess. It's just that I keep seeing eyes like his everywhere I look. The bus driver. His eyes are orange, too."

"Alicia, I really think that—"

The boarding announcement for our flight to Inverness came through the loudspeaker. I smiled and squeezed her arm. "Come on," I said. "We're flying away from madmen with orange eyes. No one in Scotland has orange eyes. Trust me."

The flight was uneventful, landing in Inverness right on schedule. I would have enjoyed spending some time in the city, but our bus was waiting, a handsome vehicle staffed by an attendant who served coffee, cocktails, and soft drinks along with a variety of sandwiches. The driver was a portly gentleman with a ready smile and a brogue that sounded like a foreign language.

We headed north, crossing a bridge that spanned the waters of Beauly Firth, continued across Black Isle until reaching another bridge above Cromarty Firth, took various roads until getting on to the A9 Highway that ran along the eastern coast of Scotland, passing through towns called Golspie and Brora, Helmsdale and Blackness, until eventually coming to the outer limits of Wick.

"Here we are," I said, my heart beating a little

faster at the contemplation of having reached our destination. Of course, there was additional glee for me. After years of invitations from George Sutherland to visit the castle in which he'd been brought up, I would finally be there.

Dusk had started to fall as we proceeded in the direction of Sutherland Castle, hugging the most spectacular coastline I'd ever seen—and Maine's coast is among the most beautiful in the world.

But this was different. The cliffs soared high above the swirling sea, rugged, sheer drops of hundreds of feet. A stiff wind whipped the trees into a frenzied dance, and flocks of birds erupted into the air from their nesting grounds in the rocks—great northern divers, redshanks, snipes, and skylarks.

Our driver went slowly along the very edge of the bluffs, creating a sensation that we might topple over at any moment. Then, as a fast-moving black cloud passed what was left of the orange sun, allowing its copper rays to burst forth, Sutherland Castle was in my view, standing starkly alone on the highest cliff, the angry sky its imposing scrim. An involuntary gasp came from everyone on the bus. It was a sight none of us would forget for the rest of our lives.

Dominating the stone structure was a tower house rising three or four stories, with a pair of corbeled two-story angle turrets. Additions to the tower house jutted out in all directions, some two stories high, some only one story. Windows appeared to have been included haphazardly, although the narrow slits in the tower house had symmetry to them.

As the bus came closer to the castle, some of the exterior perimeter grounds came into view—chestnut trees, rowans and hollies, lilacs and rhododendrons.

We entered between two huge stone lions and beneath a masonry arch, and were inside the compound: a broad, grassy area with a gravel drive. I peered through the window and saw George standing on stone steps that led up to a pair of massive wooden front doors, each six feet wide. I blinked and looked again. He was wearing a kilt, and waist-length black formal jacket over a white shirt.

The sound of bagpipes filled the courtyard, and a kilted piper emerged from behind a column, the unwieldy instrument cradled in his arms.

It had been a happy journey on the bus. But now the excitement level surged as we prepared to exit the vehicle. I held back, and was the last of our group to descend the stairs and plant my feet on Sutherland Castle's turf. Others in the party had greeted George and surrounded him. When he saw me, he left them, extended his arms to me, and said, "Welcome, fair lassie."

I grinned, looked left and right, and said, "You were born and raised in *this*?"

"Afraid so."

"You certainly weren't cramped for space."

"No. But the winters were a wee bit chilly. Come, Jessica. Make yourself at home."

Three men of varying ages came from behind the castle to unload our luggage as George led us inside. The entrance hall was the size of my living room in Cabot Cove. The floor was gray stone. Persian kilim rugs hung on the walls. The furniture was large and heavy; a Louis XV commode with an oyster veneer, a pair of splay-back chairs, and a huge pendulum clock.

"It's breathtaking," Susan Shevlin said, making notes. She always took notes wherever she traveled in order to provide firsthand information to her travel agency clients.

Mort Metzger and Seth Hazlitt went to the foot of the stairs leading to an upper level and looked up them. "What's up there?" Mort asked.

"Your rooms," George replied. "But we'll get to them a little later. Your bags will be there and unpacked when we do. For now, cocktails await in the drawing room."

As we walked through other rooms and down hallways to reach the drawing room, the splendor and magnitude of the castle became increasingly obvious—and awe-inspiring. There were suits of armor, tapestries depicting Scottish history, large shields with the Sutherland Clan crest emblazoned on them. The piper was now in the drawing room and "played us in." A scarred table ran the length of one entire wall—twenty feet long. On it was a variety of food displayed on silver platters. On the opposite side of the room was an ornate Italian breakfront serving as a bar. Behind it stood a tall, stooped man wearing kilts and a black turtleneck sweater that had seen better days. He had a full head of greasy black hair that he'd slicked back, but its naturally unruly nature won out. His face was long and craggy, his eyes almost the color of his sweater. I glanced to where Jed and Alicia Richardson stood. Jed was beaming with delight at his surroundings; the look on his wife's face said something else.

"Alicia," I said softly, coming to her side and casually placing my arm over her shoulder. "Everything is fine."

"That man," she muttered. "The bartender."

"Yes?"

"I don't like him."

"He does look—well, menacing, I suppose. But I'm sure he's a perfectly nice person. Remember, he works for George, who happens to be one of Scotland Yard's top people. George would never hire anyone he didn't implicitly trust."

"I know, I know," she said. "I'm being silly."

She managed a smile. "Don't worry about me, Jess. Go on, get a drink and some food."

Jed Richardson was already at the table putting salmon and trout, oysters with lemon, brown bread and wild game pâté on a plate. "Jed," I said, "keep an eye on Alicia."

He turned to me. "You noticed, huh?"

"Hard not to. She's really shaken from your experience in London."

"I know. But she'll be okay. This place is so great, Jess. It'll put her at ease. Your friend, George, is some guy. Must be richer than a king, huh?"

"Not at all," I said. "He was left this castle, but that was all he was left. He has to run it as a hotel just to keep it up and pay the taxes."

"Why doesn't he sell it?"

"He says he's considered that often, but can't bring himself to do it. A lot of sentimental value, which I can understand. At any rate, keep tabs on Alicia. I want her to enjoy this."

Ken Sassi joined us. "When do we fish?" he asked.

"I'll ask George about that. In the meantime, you've found the food. Enjoy."

I took a few items of food, and a soft drink from the scowling bartender, and managed to corner George away from the others.

"Enjoying yourself, Jess?" he asked.

"How could I not? I wish I'd taken you up on your invitation years ago, and that I had a few months to spend here. I've never been in a castle before. A real one, I mean. And it's the first time I've seen your knees."

His warm, gentle laugh made me feel good. "Not an especially inspiring sight, I'm afraid. I come from a long but proud family in which bow-legs prevail. You're right about the castle. It is real, all right. And haunted, they say."

"Stop it," I said. I lowered my voice. "And please don't say that to Alicia Richardson. She's still trying to get over her experience with that crazy man."

"I understand. Is the food to your liking?"

"It's wonderful. Haunted?"

"According to some folks."

"Your relative, the descendant of that witch, Isa-bell Gowdie? Is she this supposed ghost?"

"I think so."

"Have *you* ever seen this ghost?"

"No."

"What do others say she looks like?"

"A lovely lady dressed all in white. But with a cross carved into her throat. The blood sometimes runs from the slashes and down over the front of her white gown. Sometimes it doesn't. She has orange eyes."

"It's cold in here," I said.

"I'll get you a sweater."

"No thank you. No need. An internal chill."

"I'm so glad you're here, Jess. We must find some time together—alone. To talk."

"I look forward to that, George. I think I'd better mingle with my friends. They consider me their tour guide."

"I can't think of a better one."

"By the way, Ken Sassi—he's the fishing guide—wants to know when he and I can find a day on the stream."

"I'll check with the gillie."

"Gillie?"

"Fishing guide. We call them gillies. There's a few good ones in town. I'll check out where they're biting, what sort of bait to use, that sort of thing."

"We don't use bait," I said. "We use artificial flies."

"Sorry, but I don't fish. Excuse the inaccurate nomenclature. I'll let you and Ken know first thing in the morning."

Eventually, we went to our rooms. Mine was in the front of the castle overlooking the central courtyard. It was a magnificent suite, large and airy, with a fireplace already blazing, a canopied king-size bed, old original oil paintings on the walls, massive antique furniture, and a small mural stair leading up to a cramped room barely high enough to stand up straight.

The bathroom featured an enameled copper bath and one small continental commode, as well as a large French provincial armoire, and an English serpentine-fronted chest of drawers.

"Heavenly," I said aloud as I took it all in. My bags had been unpacked, and everything was neatly hung in the armoire. A large basket of fruit and sweets and a bottle of champagne were tempting.

I spent a half hour gazing out the window. It was now dark; small exterior lamps cast tiny pools of light over the front door and along the gravel drive.

I freshened up and dressed for dinner. Pleased with the way I looked, I left my room and ventured down the long, wide hallway leading to the stairs. When I reached them, I stopped to admire a painting on the wall. As I did, a stream of very cold air touched my skin. I turned to see whether a window had suddenly been opened. That's when I saw her, a tall, beautiful woman dressed all in white. She stood in the hallway staring at me with eyes the color of copper.

"Hello?" I said softly.

That's when I saw the red stain growing on the bodice of her gown.

I gasped.

"Gie a heize." The voice was soft and low, ethereal.

"What?" I said.
She was gone.
"Wait," I said.
I was alone in the hallway.

Chapter Five

"Are you all right, Jessica?" Seth Hazlitt asked when I walked into the dining room. "You're as pale as a sheet."

"I'm—I'm all right, Seth. It's just that—"

"Yes?"

"Nothing. I thought I saw something that obviously wasn't there."

"Seein' things, are you?"

I smiled. "A sign of advancing age?" I looked around the huge dining room. "Looks like you and I are the first."

"*Ayuh.* Seems that way."

The dining room defined splendor. It was paneled in cherry wood; an ornate Italian frieze ran the upper circumference, twenty feet above. Huge oil portraits of George's ancestors dominated each wall. The floor was covered in thick Persian carpets. The table, set for seventeen, provided a dazzling display of silver, china, and linen.

A door opened, and George stepped into the room, followed by two couples. George looked splendid in his Sutherland clan kilt of greens, white, and red, and black waistcoat, fluted white shirt, black bow tie, and knee-high black socks. A crest on the jacket's lapel showed two men in loincloths with crude clubs flanking a shield. George explained later in the evening that the motto on his clan shield, SANS PEUR, meant "Without fear."

"Jessica, Dr. Hazlitt," George said, "allow me to introduce our other guests at the castle. This is Mr. and Mrs. Brock Peterman. And this is Dr. and Mrs. Geoffrey Symington."

Brock Peterman and his wife, Tammy, seemed very out of place in this Scottish castle. Both had deep tans. Her hair was silver blond, and there was lots of it. His black hairpiece was obvious; it had a plastic look to it. She wore a skintight white dress that clung to every curve of her youthful, voluptuous body. He wore a yellow sport jacket over a black T-shirt, green slacks, and tasseled brown alligator loafers, no socks.

"Brock is a movie producer from Hollywood," George said after we'd greeted each other.

"Oh? Might *I* have seen any of your films?" I asked.

"If you like quality horror flicks," he said,

flashing a mouthful of large, perfect white teeth. *"The Reptile's Revenge*? That's my latest."

"I'm afraid I missed it," I said.

Dr. Geoffrey Symington was a short, thin man in his midforties, with a hawk's nose and deeply set green eyes. His wife, Helen, was a few inches taller than her husband, and considerably wider. They were appropriately dressed for the occasion: a black tuxedo for him, a sequined floor-length gown for her.

"What sort a' medicine do you practice, Dr. Symington?" Seth asked.

"Research," he replied.

"What sort a' research?"

"Basic. Excuse me. I left something in my room."

As Seth raised his eyebrows at me, the door again opened and others from our group arrived. After introductions had been made, we took our assigned seats at the table.

Two people served us. One was the brooding, stooped black-eyed man who'd been our bartender during the cocktail hour. The other was a young woman with a sweet, ruddy round face wearing an old-fashioned floor-length gray dress that buttoned tight around her neck. She struck me as one of those fortunate women who would always look the same, no matter how old she became.

The menu was elaborate: Nettle soup to start. Next, a wonderful salmon roe pâté, then a main course of stuffed trout caught that day on a local stream, and accompanied by "stovies," a special seed potato cooked with onions. Dessert was "whipt syllabub," a whipped concoction served with homemade macaroons. Charlene Sassi, Cabot Cove's resident baking genius, pronounced them the best she'd ever tasted.

As the evening progressed, the conversation turned to rumors that Sutherland Castle was haunted.

"Is it?" Susan Shevlin asked George. "Is it really haunted?"

George laughed and told our waiter to refill everyone's wineglass. "Perhaps we should ask Mr. Peterman that question," he said. "He's here researching his next movie."

"A ghost story?" Charlene Sassi asked.

"A sci-fi horror flick with a ghost subplot," Peterman said. "I figure it needs a castle setting, so when I read about this place being open to guests, I told Tammy to call the travel agent."

"You're going to shoot your new movie here, at this castle?" radio station owner Peter Walters asked.

"Depends," Peterman said. "I keep telling Mr. Sutherland how much business my movie can generate for his hotel. But he—"

"Afraid this Scotsman is having trouble understanding why I should pay in order to have Mr. Peterman make his movie here," George said, keeping his tone light. "I thought it worked the other way around. *You* pay *me* for using my castle as your set."

"It's marketing," Peterman said. "You need to market this place. The movie would be great. Bring in lots of business. Right, Tammy?"

His wife, who hadn't said much during dinner, appeared to be on the verge of dozing off. She snapped to attention and said, "Yes. Absolutely."

"Have you found *real* ghosts here?" Susan Shevlin asked the moviemaker.

He shook his head and downed his wine. "Nah. No such thing. The only ghosts and ghouls are the ones my special effects people create."

All the talk of ghosts and ghouls caused me to look to Alicia Richardson, who seemed to be in a trance, staring straight ahead, unblinking, her pretty face an expressionless mask.

"Jessica says she saw something on her way down to dinner," Seth, who sat to my right, said. "Might have been a ghost."

"Was it, Jess?" Roberta Walters asked. The array of wines served during and after dinner had obviously gone to her head. She giggled like a schoolgirl.

I looked again at Alicia, who didn't seem to have heard what was being said.

"What *did* you see, Jess?" Susan Shevlin asked.

"I didn't see anything," I said. "I thought I did but—"

"An apparition?" Dr. Symington said in a low voice. He hadn't spoken since sitting down for dinner.

I tried to change the subject out of deference to Alicia Richardson, but the others seemed determined to continue discussing ghosts.

"Do you know anything about the supernatural?" Seth Hazlitt asked Symington.

"A bit," he replied.

"Is that your research?" Seth continued. "Into apparitions?"

"It is a particular interest of mine," the doctor replied.

"Doesn't sound like anything a medical doctor would get involved in," said Seth. That he didn't particularly like Dr. Symington had been evident all evening.

"A matter of opinion," Symington said. "There is much medical science can learn from the unexplained." His accent was clipped British. "Traditional medicine has operated with blinders on." He turned to the young serving woman standing in a corner awaiting further orders. "More wine!" he commanded. His wife, Helen, who'd been a pleasant dinner companion, placed her hand on her husband's arm and said, "Perhaps you shouldn't, Geoff." He scowled at her and held up his glass for the serving girl's benefit.

Brock Peterman abruptly stood, and urged his wife to her feet. "Excuse us," he said. "We need a walk, some fresh air." Tammy Peterman walked unsteadily behind her husband, who seemed angry about something.

When they were gone, Mort Metzger said, "Strange pair."

"From Hollywood," George offered in way of explanation.

"What did you see, Mrs. Fletcher?" Dr. Symington asked in his characteristically low monotone.

"Pardon?"

"You said you saw something earlier this evening. I suggested it was an apparition. Was it?"

I looked past him to the young serving girl, who seemed upset by the conversation. George saw her, too, and said, "I think we're finished here, Daisy. Forbes will take care of after-dinner drinks in the drawing room. You're excused."

Daisy didn't hesitate to take George up on his offer to leave. She was gone instantly, leaving the stooped man named Forbes to continue serving us.

An elaborate array of after-dinner liqueurs had been set up in the drawing room. After Forbes had served me a glass of seltzer, I found myself cornered by Dr. Symington. "You were saying," he said, managing what passed for a smile.

"Saying about what, Doctor?"

"What you saw. The apparition."

"That's your assumption," I said sweetly. "I never said I saw an apparition."

"But I gather you did. The lady in the white dress?"

My gasp was involuntary and audible. "You've seen her?" I said.

He sipped his green liqueur. "Then, you *have* seen her, Mrs. Fletcher."

George suddenly appeared at my side. "Mind if I steal her away for a few minutes, Dr. Symington?" he asked.

"Of course not. This is your castle, Mr. Sutherland. You do what you wish."

"A little air?" George said in my ear. "You look pale."

"I'd love a little air."

Everyone else seemed to be enjoying themselves, chatting and drinking. George's hand on my elbow guided me from the room, down the hallway, and out a small door leading to the outdoors. The sweet night air filled my nostrils. Above, a full moon came and went behind fast-moving clouds.

"What a pretty courtyard," I said. We were in

a small area enclosed on four sides by stone walls. We sat on a stone bench.

"My favorite respite," George said. "When I need to think about something, I usually come out here."

"I can see why. It must be lovely in the daytime."

"Yes, it is. Jess, what was this thing you saw before coming down for dinner?"

"The lady in white."

"Oh."

"I would have dismissed it as nothing more than the result of travel fatigue. I didn't even want to mention it. But then Dr. Symington asked whether I'd seen a woman in white. I did. And you say there is such a woman."

"Not that I can personally attest to. Others claim to have seen her. That doesn't mean she exists."

"But Dr. Symington just told me he's seen her. And I have. That's got to be more than sheer coincidence, George."

"Perhaps. But I don't believe in ghosts."

"Nor do I. You're the chief inspector. How do you explain so many witnesses having seen her?"

"I have no explanation for it, Jessica. The power of suggestion perhaps. Tell me not to think of purple elephants, and that's all I'll think of. I do know one thing."

"Which is?"

"That whoever—whatever this strange female creature in white is, she's becoming a bloody *pyne* in my neck."

"I take it you mean 'pain.' "

"Exactly. Ever since she started making her appearances, I keep losing staff. Having the right people here is crucial, Jessica, because I'm so seldom here. I depend upon the staff to keep things running smoothly, satisfy the guests, maintain the property. But I've lost my best people recently and have had to settle."

I thought of Alicia Richardson's apprehension about Forbes, the bartender, and my assurances to her that George would never hire anyone in whom he didn't have the utmost faith. Maybe I was wrong.

We sat in silence for a minute, each of us occupied with our own thoughts. I broke the silence. "George, has anyone who claims to have seen the woman in white reported her having spoken to them?"

He frowned. "No. Can't say that I have."

"She spoke to me."

He turned on the bench so that we faced each other. "She did? What did she say?"

"I don't know. I mean, I don't remember. I didn't recognize the words, couldn't even begin to repeat them to you."

"Words? More than one?"

"Yes. A phrase, a sentence. Short, but definitely more than a single word."

"Interesting."

"I was probably just hearing things."

"Yes. That's undoubtedly what happened."

"We should get back to the others," I said, standing.

"I suppose so," he said, also getting up from the bench. "I trust you know that this brief conversation will not count toward our spending some time alone. I don't intend to squander those moments discussing nonsense like ghosts."

"You're right," I said.

"I thought perhaps we could steal off for a day while the others sightsee. I'll take you on a personal tour of Wick and its surroundings. We'll have lunch in my favorite pub. Just the two of us. Time alone."

"I'd like that," I said. "Come. They'll be wondering where we've gone."

Dr. Symington tried to engage me in more conversation about the woman in white, but I managed to deflect his questions and surround myself with friends from Cabot Cove. The after-dinner gathering eventually broke up, and we headed for our rooms.

"Sleep tight, Mrs. F.," Mort Metzger said. "Busy day tomorrow."

"It is?" I said.

"Didn't get the itinerary? Goin' to get to see lots a' the countryside. Early breakfast. Seven."

"I'll be up and ready," I said.

George walked me to the head of the stairs. "Everything all right, Jessica?" he asked.

"Oh, yes, and will continue to be as long as I don't bump into the lady in white again."

"Chances are slim that will happen. People who've reported seeing her say it's a onetime event."

"I'm pleased to hear that. Well, good night, George. Thanks for a wonderful welcome to Sutherland Castle. See you at breakfast?"

"Absolutely. Go on, run along. I have some paperwork to do before getting to bed. I'm happy you're here, Jessica. Very happy indeed."

He walked away and disappeared through a door. I looked up the wide, carpeted staircase but didn't take my first step. Instead, I narrowed my eyes to better pierce the shadowed upstairs landing. Silly, I thought, starting up. George said you only see her once. Besides, I never even saw her the first time. He was right: It was all a matter of our power of suggestion. Purple elephants. I saw them as I continued to ascend the staircase, and smiled.

I reached the top, paused, and said in a whisper, "Hello? Are you there?"

No reply.

"Hello?" I repeated. "If you decide to show yourself again, I suggest—"

"You all right, Jessica?"

I turned to face Seth Hazlitt, who stood in the door of his room.

"Of course."

"Who are you talkin' to?"

"Talking to? I wasn't talking to anyone."

"Thought I heard you talkin' to someone. Must've been my imagination."

"Must have been. Good night, Seth."

It took a long time to fall asleep. I heard every sound in the castle, and outside noises, too. A wind came up and rattled the windows. A clock chimed the hour from somewhere in the castle. An occasional door slammed shut. Female voices, loud at first, then fading away.

Ghosts, indeed!

The last thing I heard before drifting off were the voices of two men outside and below my window. They sounded angry. Then they faded away, too.

And so did I.

Chapter Six

According to my *American Heritage Dictionary*, the term "dour" means marked by sternness or harshness; forbidding; silently ill-humored; gloomy; sternly obstinate; unyielding.

Those descriptive words and others accurately described Mary Gower, Sutherland Castle's cook. A short, solidly constructed woman, she served us a breakfast of bacon, eggs, grilled tomato, fried bread, and kippers—herring from Loch Fyne, split open and cooked over oak chips—with grinding efficiency, plates set down with conviction, and taken away the moment the last morsel had been consumed. Throughout, never a smile was cracked or a word spoken.

"Wouldn't want to get on her bad side," Seth Hazlitt muttered to George Sutherland.

George laughed. "Yes, Mrs. Gower does tend to fall on the dour side," he said.

Which caused me to laugh. "A Scottish understatement," I said.

"A good woman," George said. "A hard life. Her husband was one of Wick's last herring fishermen." He pronounced Wick "Week," a throwback to the days when the Vikings occupied it. "The Scandinavians came back in the sixties with their big, modern boats and scooped up all the herring. Set the town on hard times. Wick was once the herring capital of the world. Mr. Gower died at sea, like so many of the village's citizens over the years."

"She cooks good," Mort Metzger said.

"Which is why I put up with her lack of—what shall I say?—her lack of charm?" George said.

After breakfast, we gathered in the central courtyard, where a small bus waited to take those of us who wished to go on a tour of the area. Forbes, the castle's brooding jack-of-all-trades, was the driver.

"Not coming with us?" Jed Richardson asked me as he and Alicia were about to board.

"No. I think I'll spend the day relaxing," I said.

"Us, too," said Jim Shevlin, Cabot Cove's newly elected mayor. "I thought I'd wander down to town hall, see how government works here."

The Petermans hadn't come to breakfast; Peter and Roberta Walters had left word they were skipping breakfast and sleeping late.

I watched the bus pull away, went inside, and settled in an oversize, overstuffed chair in front of a massive fireplace in which thin logs piled against each other vertically sent a welcome warmth into the room. Although it was springtime, there was a distinct chill in the air, as well as in the castle. A young man wearing a kilt, whom I'd seen only when he had helped bring our luggage into the castle upon our arrival, appeared and asked if I wanted tea.

"That would be wonderful," I said. "Hot tea and a warm fire. Perfect."

When he delivered the tea, he lingered, as though wanting to say something.

"How long have you worked at Sutherland Castle?" I asked to break the silence.

"Just a month, ma'am."

"It must be an interesting place to work."

"That it is. Mr. Sutherland is a good boss. When he's here."

"Who's in charge when he isn't here?" I asked.

"Mrs. Gower sometimes. Forbes. Depends. I don't wish to seem bold, ma'am, but I understand you write murder mysteries."

"Yes, I do."

"So do I."

"Really? How many have you written?"

"Only one. Been working on it for a year, on and off you might say. When I have the time."

"Is it set here, in Wick? *Week*, I mean."

His youthful smile was pleasant. "Yes, ma'am.

It's about a real murder that happened here twenty years ago, right in the village."

"Twenty years ago. That wouldn't be the relative of Isabell Gowdie, would it?"

"You know about that?" His voice went up in pitch to mirror his surprise.

"Yes. Mr. Sutherland told me about it."

"I was only three years old at the time," he said. "But my mother talked about it a great deal. Kept all the newspaper stories and the like."

"Fascinating. Could I read it while I'm here?"

"That's what I wanted to ask you to do, ma'am, only I thought it might be rude, considering you're a famous writer and all."

"I'd be delighted to read your book."

He left, returning moments later carrying a small leather backpack from which he withdrew a tattered, dog-eared one-hundred-page manuscript. The title was *Who Killed Evelyn Gowdie?* Right to the point.

"Did they ever find out who murdered this Evelyn Gowdie?" I asked, thumbing through the pages.

"No, ma'am. That's the murder mystery part of my book. I have my detective solve the real murder."

"An interesting approach," I said, "combining fact and fiction."

I was about to ask other questions when Mrs.

Gower appeared in the doorway and said sternly, "Get back to your chores, Malcolm, and stop botherin' the guests."

"That's all right," I said.

She ignored me. "Come on, now, get to work. You're the laziest boy I've ever seen. Dreamin' all day about foolish books, and Daisy not showin' up, just as lazy as you. Can't rely on any young person these days."

Malcolm—I now knew his first name—grabbed his backpack and scurried from the room, Mrs. Gower's harsh stare following him all the way. I started to say something in his defense, but all I saw was the broad back of our cook as she turned away and lumbered down the hall, her heavy footsteps ringing off the stone floor.

I sipped my tea and read Malcolm's first chapter, which succinctly laid out for the reader the bare facts of Evelyn Gowdie's murder twenty years ago. She was the woman who George claimed was a descendant of the famed Scottish witch, Isabell Gowdie, put to death in 1622 by a pitchfork through her heart, and a cross slashed into the flesh of her throat. According to Malcolm's manuscript, Evelyn Gowdie's body had been found behind a small office building on Bridge Street, Wick's main thoroughfare.

I decided to put off reading more of the manuscript until later in the day, and went to my room, where I changed into new sneakers and a green-and-white jogging suit over another layer of clothing. Confident I'd dressed appropriately for whatever weather I might encounter—George said the weather in northern Scotland could change within minutes—I left the castle and walked in the direction of the village.

It took me longer than I'd planned to reach Bridge Street because I kept stopping to admire the rugged natural beauty of the area. The sun shone brightly, providing its warm rays to the crisp morning. There were spectacular rock formations along the tops of the cliffs that George had said were called "Grey Bools"; a soaring natural arch in those same cliffs, "Brig o'Trams," made a bold, awe-inspiring statement against the cobalt blue sky.

I eventually reached the center of town and paused on a corner to get my bearings. Not that Wick was large enough for a tourist to become lost. What struck me as I stood on the corner was the absence of people. There were a few men and women walking down Bridge Street, going in and out of shops. But there weren't many shops to enter, at least from my vantage point. Some were boarded up, others had CLOSED signs on their doors. Overall, the impression was of a village that had not only fallen on hard times in the past, those hard times prevailed to this day. That impression was enhanced when the sun ceased to shine, as though someone had thrown a switch, and a cold rain started to fall. I'd heard about "horizontal rain" in northern Scotland; now I experienced it. A wind that suddenly began to howl down Bridge Street flung the raindrops in a horizontal direction, stinging my face and sending me in search of shelter. I found it in a small shop selling sporting goods, guns and ammunition, fishing rods and artificial lures. An older man was behind the counter as I entered, causing a tiny bell attached to the door to sound.

"*Guid* morning," he said.

"Good morning. Goodness, that rain came up fast."

He laughed. "Another few minutes, the sun will be shining brightly again."

"So I've heard."

"Something I can help you with?"

"I only came in to stay dry. But now that I'm here, maybe you would give me some advice on what dry flies to use, what the fish are rising to."

The shopkeeper spent the next fifteen minutes showing me various dry flies, which, he proudly proclaimed, he'd tied himself. I bought a few. By the time I'd paid, the sun was out and the rain had stopped.

I left the store and slowly walked up Bridge Street, pausing to peer into shop windows, and observing the few people sharing the street with me. It didn't take long to reach the end, where the village just seemed to fade into a country road.

I turned back and headed in the direction from which I'd come. As I started back down Bridge Street, a small sign on an office building caught my eye. I moved closer to read it. It was a plaque that had been placed on the building by the Wick Historical Society. It read: *"Site of the murder of Evelyn Gowdie, Feb. 11, 1976, descendant of famed Scottish witch, Isabell Gowdie."*

A strange thing to commemorate.

I stepped away from the building, but something caused me to go back and read the plaque again. Well, I thought, since the leaders of the Wick Historical Society felt a woman's murder was worth a plaque, I might as well see where it actually happened.

There was a dirt driveway running from the street to the rear of the building. I walked along it until reaching a backyard area strewn with bottles and other trash. Weeds grew with abandon. I looked at the building's rear windows; no one looked back. I wondered whether a second plaque had been installed, pinpointing precisely where the body was discovered. I didn't see one.

I was poised to leave when my attention was drawn to a large cardboard box in a corner of the small yard. To be more precise, it was what protruded from the end of the box closest to me that was of interest.

I went to it, and my initial reaction was validated. It was a foot, a female foot wearing a high black laced-up shoe. A few inches of ankle showed between the shoe's top and the hem of a gray dress. I hesitated; I wanted to push the box aside but had difficulty mustering the courage.

Then, after a few deep breaths, I used my foot to partially slide the box off the body, enough to see the face belonging to the foot and leg. Looking up at me was the round, ruddy face of Daisy—I didn't know her last name—the young woman who'd served us dinner the night before at Sutherland Castle.

My fist went to my mouth to stifle an anguished cry about to erupt. A pitchfork rose from Daisy's chest. The handle had been broken off just above the metal tines. Brown dried blood surrounded each tooth.

I crouched lower. I hadn't seen it at first glance. Carved into her throat was a small, bloody cross.

I quickly retraced my steps to the street and looked up and down. I wanted to scream, but held that impulse in check. Instead, I went to the sporting goods shop.

"Forget something?" the owner asked.

"No. There's been a murder up the street. Behind the office building where Evelyn Gowdie was killed twenty years ago."

He looked at me skeptically.

"It's a young girl named Daisy. She works—worked at Sutherland Castle."

"Daisy Wemyss?"

"I don't know her last name. All I know is that—"

"Come with me," he said, leading me from the store. "She's my brother's daughter."

Chapter Seven

The shop owner led me to a small building in which Wick's government offices were housed. We stepped into a room marked CONSTABLE, where a young man sat reading a newspaper, his feet propped on the edge of the desk.

"Bob," the shop owner said. "We've got a big problem down the street."

Bob looked up. "Oh?"

"There's been a murder. Daisy, my brother's girl."

Bob dropped the newspaper to the desk, his feet to the floor.

"Where's Horace?"

"Down to the river fishing."

"Well, go get the man. Fast." The shop owner turned to me. "Where did you find her body?"

I explained.

"Who's she?" Bob asked.

"I'm Jessica Fletcher. I'm a guest at Sutherland Castle. I found her."

"Go on, Bob, get Horace." To me: "Horace is our constable."

Bob ran from the office.

"I take it your name is Mr. Wemyss," I said to the shop owner.

"Ay."

"What do we do now? Wait for the constable to return from fishing?"

"Best thing to do."

"Isn't there someone else we can talk to?"

"Best to wait for Horace."

Another dour Scotsman, I thought. I'd better get used to it.

Horace, whose last name turned out to be McKay, arrived ten minutes later carrying the longest fishing rod I'd ever seen. He wore "Wellies," green rubber boots seen everywhere in Great Britain, and had with him a creel containing two large trout. After I'd been introduced to him, he said, "Now, lady, what's this about Daisy Wemyss?"

"She's been murdered." I told him where I'd discovered the body.

"Back where Evelyn Gowdie was killed," he said in a low, gruff voice, heavy with Scottish burr.

"That's right," I said. "I suggest we go there—now!" I was running out of patience with their cavalier approach to murder. Mr. Wemyss's niece had been brutally killed. Constable McKay had a murder on his hands. But here they were standing around as though we were discussing the fish he'd caught.

"Let's go," said McKay. He carefully placed the rod on wall hooks behind his desk, took off his wide-brimmed hat and patted his hair flat in front of a tiny mirror, put his hat back on, and led us from the office.

We stood in a circle over the lifeless body of Daisy Wemyss. Constable McKay knelt next to the body and touched his fingertips to her neck. He looked up at us: "She's been dead for some time," he said. "Ten, twelve hours."

"The pitchfork," I said. "And the cross on her neck. The same as Evelyn Gowdie."

Constable McKay stood, stretched, and grimaced against a pain somewhere in his body. "You know about that," he said to me.

"Yes, I do."

McKay turned to Mr. Wemyss and said, "You'd better inform your brother."

"*Ay*. Not a pleasant task."

"If it's all right," I said, "I'd like to go back to Sutherland Castle."

"By all means," McKay said. "How long will you be staying there?"

"Another week."

"Good. I'll be wanting to speak with you again."

"I look forward to it, Constable. I'm sorry for your loss, Mr. Wemyss."

"Nothing guaranteed in this life, Mrs. Fletcher. Dying is the price we pay for living."

"I'll inform George Sutherland and the others at the castle about Ms. Wemyss's death."

"Do that," said Constable McKay.

I went to the street and slowly made my way back to Sutherland Castle, looming on the horizon, a bleak stone bastion of the ages rising imposingly over the modest village of Wick, Scotland.

I quickened my pace, legs aching as I climbed the steep incline leading to my home for the next week. George was on the lawn pruning a bush.

"Pleasant walk?" he asked, placing the pruning shears in the jacket of a tan vest.

"No."

"Sorry to hear that, Jessica. Why?"

I told him about Daisy Wemyss.

His face turned hard and ashen.

"George. What's going on here?"

"I don't know, Jessica, but it's obvious there's a madman out there."

"The same one who killed Evelyn Gowdie twenty years ago?"

" 'And from his wallet drew a human hand, shriveled and dry and black. . . .' "

"What?"

" 'And fitting, as he spoke, a taper in his

hold . . . pursued a murderer on this stake had died. . . .' "

"George."

"Southey. He wrote it in *Thalabra*. A popular belief centuries ago that the hand of a man executed for murder, if prepared properly, could cast a perpetual spell over future generations."

George Sutherland was fond of quoting ancient passages, and had a remarkable memory for them.

"You don't believe in such things, do you, George?"

"I believe in good and evil, Jessica. Come. If spells can be cast over evil doers, I intend to try my best to cast one myself. This was *not* what I intended when inviting you and your friends to my family home."

Chapter Eight

George and I sat in front of the fireplace where I'd enjoyed tea that morning. When he informed the cook, Mrs. Gower, of Daisy Wemyss's death, the shocking news didn't appear to shock her. She muttered something about young people asking for trouble these days before flouncing off to fetch us tea and scones.

After serving us, George said, "I'm so sorry about this, Jessica."

"Please, George, don't be. It wasn't anything you could have prevented."

"I'm not certain that's true."

"Why do you say that?"

"It's hard to explain, Jessica. There's really nothing tangible to account for it, just a lot of Scottish lore involving my family, this castle, and Wick itself."

"I'll do my best to understand," I said.

"Yes, I'm sure you will."

He tasted his tea. I offered the plate of scones to him, but he shook his head.

"Let me see where to begin," he said thoughtfully. "It started centuries ago, when this castle was built by my ancestors. They were a staunch, fearless people. 'Without fear' is our clan motto."

"I saw that on the shield."

"A proud clan, Jessica. A proud people. But from the beginning, the existence of this castle was viewed by some with skepticism, even outright hostility."

"Why, for heaven's sake?"

"Rumor. Superstition. Fear. Envy. Hatred."

"Directed toward your family?"

"Yes."

"Again, I ask why?"

"Because it has been believed since the day my family built this remarkable place that it's been occupied not only by members of the Sutherland Clan, but by—well, by ghosts."

I couldn't help but laugh. "Like the lady in white?" I asked.

"Were it only about her, Jessica. No, over the centuries the people of Wick have blamed the castle and its occupants for almost every violent act occurring in the village." He drew a deep breath. "I should have told you all of this before inviting you and your friends."

"Don't be silly. Some people in Wick might

think there's some brand of witchcraft being practiced at Sutherland Castle, but I'm certainly not
one of them. Nor are any of my friends."

"Mrs. Richardson?"

"Alicia? I can understand why she's still upset.
That incident at the Tower of London would leave
anyone shaken."

"Of course. But I can't help but wonder whether
that incident wasn't preordained in some way.
After all, the man who held her and her husband
wanted to salvage the name of a distant relative
accused of practicing witchcraft."

"Sheer coincidence," I said, putting a dollop of
clotted cream on my scone and taking a bite.

"Yes. But then we have Isabell Gowdie being
murdered over three hundred years ago, put to
death as a witch by a pitchfork in the chest, and
a cross carved in her throat. Flash-forward to
twenty years ago. Evelyn Gowdie killed the same
way. And now, twenty years later, Daisy Wemyss.
Sheer coincidence?"

"No. Of course not. But it has nothing to do
with you or this castle."

"Intellect versus emotion, Jessica. Intellectually,
you're right. No connection at all. But emotion-
ally? Well, it's hard to not wonder whether there's
some sort of mystical link, no matter how vague
or tangential."

"I suggest you stick with your keenly honed intellect, George. You wear it well."

"You're right, of course, as usual. You mentioned earlier that Constable McKay seemed angry when he mentioned my name."

"Yes, I sensed that."

"I'm not surprised."

"Why?"

"He's a good man, Jessica. But he's between, as the saying goes, a rock and a hard place. Whenever something violent happens in Wick, he's buffeted between two forces—the reasonable citizens of the village, and another group that has carried forward this distrust of the Sutherland clan and Sutherland Castle. This latter group is very superstitious, steeped in old mythology and metaphor. In their eyes, every problem will be solved when and if I sell this castle."

"How would that help anything?"

"It wouldn't, at least not in the eyes of rational people. But the others believe that the only way to break the curse this castle supposedly casts over Wick is for the last surviving member of my family, namely me, to shed any connection to this place and leave."

"Are you considering that, George?"

"Yes, although not for that reason. I've mentioned to you how difficult it is to hang on to this castle. It costs a bloody fortune, and finding the right help to keep it going as a hotel has become increasingly difficult."

"So you said."

"I should. Sell it, that is. I visit here only a few weeks a year. London is my home and has been ever since I joined the Yard. But each time I come close to putting it on the market, there's a bond with my ancestors that keeps me from going through with it."

"I can certainly understand that. Is there a market for such a place?"

He smiled, his first since settling in front of the fireplace. "It's hardly a place a family of four would want to buy as a home. But its value as a hotel is considerable. There have been two investor groups that have made offers over the past few years. Sizable offers, Jessica. They see this terribly depressed area of Scotland as having tourist potential far beyond what it enjoys today."

"But you've resisted all offers."

"Yes. Foolish?"

"I don't know. Such a personal decision to make. Pragmatism versus the heart."

"Well put. I suppose I should go down to the village and pay my respects to Daisy's family. I know her father. A decent sort."

I told him about having met Daisy's uncle, the shop owner.

"I know him, too. It's a small place, although

that doesn't necessarily translate into everyone knowing everyone else. We Scots tend to stay to ourselves, especially in the smaller towns and villages."

"George, before you go, can you conceive of anyone in Wick who would have so brutally murdered Daisy Wemyss?"

"No. But after all my years with the Yard, I've come to learn that there are people—too many people—capable of such horrific acts."

We were interrupted when Malcolm entered the room. "There's someone to see you, sir."

"Who?"

"Constable McKay."

George looked at me and drew a deep breath.

"I'll be in my room," I said.

"No. Stay with me, Jessica."

Malcolm had shown the constable to a small sitting room I hadn't seen before. Another door from it led to George's office.

"Horace," George said, shaking McKay's hand. "You've met Mrs. Fletcher."

"*Ay*. And under unpleasant circumstances, I'm afraid."

"Extremely unpleasant," George said. "Please, sit down. Tea? Whiskey?"

"Whiskey. Two fingers."

George rang for Malcolm, who delivered the whiskey to Constable McKay. He drank alone.

"Well, Horace, this news about Daisy Wemyss has provided quite a shock. How is her father?"

"Unhappy."

Another Scottish understatement.

"Any leads?"

"No. George, might we have a word alone?"

"Why?"

"To discuss some of the other ramifications of this dastardly event."

"Mrs. Fletcher is aware of those other 'ramifications,' Horace. There's no need for her to leave."

"As you wish. People are beginning to hear about Daisy Wemyss, George. Some of them are threatening to take action."

"What sort of action?" I asked.

McKay gave me a hard, scolding look. I held his gaze and repeated my question.

"What they've threatened before," was McKay's answer.

I looked at George.

"They've threatened to come up here and destroy the castle," George said solemnly.

"That's terrible," I said. "But as long as they only threaten—"

"Could be they'll go further this time, miss. They're in the black mood. Daisy was a good girl, liked by everyone. Might be different if she was killed by some angry young fella who hit her, maybe even shot her. But this is the Devil speaking, George, Satan himself. Pitchfork to the chest, bloody cross carved in her young neck. Like Evelyn Gowdie before her. And the witch, Isabell."

"Excuse me," I said, "but you are the constable."

McKay looked quizzically at me.

"Surely, as Wick's top law enforcement official, you don't buy into this notion of witchcraft and Satan."

He said nothing.

"Do you?" I said.

"I can't ignore half the citizens, miss."

"Half? *Half* feel this way?"

"There's a core that do," he said. "And they're very influential. Very influential, indeed. They don't want trouble in Wick. There's been enough trouble and hard times to last everybody's lifetime."

I couldn't resist: "But you're paid to uphold the law, to keep people like this from reacting with violence."

He showed a small, sour smile, painful for him to exhibit. "Easier said than done, miss. Easier said than done."

"What are you suggesting, Horace?" asked George.

"Same thing I've suggested before, George. Sell this castle. Give it up. If you do, everything will settle down and Wick can grow. This sort of publicity, pretty young girl killed in a Devil-worship fashion, can't do the town no good. No good at all. Unless you do—I can't promise your safety, or anybody else's safety up here."

Constable McKay stood and went to the door. "No need to show me out, George. But you think about what I just said. Just announcing to the people that you plan to sell Sutherland Castle will do wonders for this town's spirits. Do wonders. Good-bye, miss."

Chapter Nine

I spent the afternoon in my room reading Mickey Spillane's new novel, *Black Alley*. I know Mickey, and am always amazed how anyone with such a sweet disposition can write best-selling tough-guy books with such authority. I've been his fan ever since his controversial first book, *I, The Jury*, was published many years ago.

At four, those who went on the tour with Forbes arrived back at the castle, and I went downstairs to greet them. They were in a jubilant mood, gushing about the natural beauty they'd seen and the lunch they'd enjoyed at an inn on the outskirts of Wick.

George had arranged for Mrs. Gower to put out a spread of salmon, caviar, and pâté to go with drinks poured by Forbes, who'd quickly traded in his bus driver's cap for a bartender's apron. Once we were gathered in the drawing room, George asked for our attention.

"I'm afraid I have some rather bad news to report," he said. "Daisy Wemyss, the young lady who worked here and served dinner last night, has been murdered."

There were the expected questions and comments.

"Jessica discovered her body this morning while walking in Wick," George said. "A tragedy, to be sure."

Now all the questions were directed at me. Where did I find her? How was she killed? Who killed her?

"Please," I said, "I really don't know any more than George has told you." I didn't want to have to go into the grisly details.

But they pressed, especially Mort Metzger, his law enforcement training coming to the fore.

"She was killed in the same fashion as the witch George wrote about in his letter to me, Isabell Gowdie. Someone rammed a pitchfork into her chest, and cut a cross on her neck."

I immediately looked to Alicia Richardson, who went pale and sat on a nearby chair. Jed stood over her, a comforting hand on her shoulder.

"Obviously, the local authorities are investigating," said George. "As dampening as this might be, we mustn't let it ruin your short stay at Sutherland Castle. I'll do everything I can to isolate you from this unpleasant and unfortunate situation.

There's no reason for it to directly impact upon your vacation."

"Easy for you to say," Seth Hazlitt said. "Wick is a small village. Could have been anyone killed the poor girl—includin' somebody workin' right here for you, Inspector Sutherland."

We all turned to the bar; Forbes was gone.

"I rather doubt that," George said. "The citizens of Wick are good and decent people, hard-working and honorable. This is the perverted work of a madman, a single individual. Don't judge all of Wick by this incident."

"Hard not to," Jim Shevlin said. "What kind of town is this? Women branded as witches, pitchforks in their chests, crosses carved in their throats. How many now? Three? That alleged witch, Isabell. Then what? Twenty years ago another woman dies that way because she's related to Isabell? And now that pretty young woman who served us dinner last night."

Shevlin addressed us: "What do all of you think? We come from Cabot Cove, a good and decent place. We bring up our kids there in peace. I ran for mayor because I wanted to keep Cabot Cove a safe place for all of us. I don't know, folks, but there's something in the air here. Something sinister. I say we pack up and leave."

I looked to George, who'd retreated to a far corner during the debate. I felt sorry for him. Obviously, none of this was his fault. He'd opened up his family home to me and my friends, and didn't deserve to be viewed as part of some wicked scheme in which women were brutally murdered.

"What do you think, Mort?" Shevlin asked our sheriff. "And you, Seth?"

Seth Hazlitt said, "Well, I think you're rushin' to judgment, Jim. I agree that this is plenty upsettin'. But just because this Miss Daisy Wemyss has been killed by a nut doesn't mean we should be packin' our bags and scurryin' out a' here."

Mort Metzger cleared his throat before saying, "I think Seth talks sense, somethin' I don't always say. But I do think that since this murder has happened right under our noses, we should keep our guard up. If you agree, I'll put together a security plan for while we're staying here at the castle."

"Security plan?" Ken Sassi said. "If we need a 'security plan,' we shouldn't be here."

An argument erupted in which everyone voiced their opinions. When their voices died down, they turned to me. "What about you, Jess?" Seth Hazlitt asked. "You're the one who suffered the shock of discoverin' the body. You're the one who invited us to come along with you to Sutherland Castle. How do you feel about stayin'?"

I glanced at George before replying. He gave me a slight shrug of his shoulders; translation—do what I thought was best without regard for him.

I said, "We're all shocked and upset at what has happened to Daisy. That's only natural and right. But to turn tail and run away from this beautiful place would be, in my judgment, an overreaction. We've had murders in Cabot Cove. That didn't cause us to run away from there."

"Because that's our home," Jed Richardson said from where he still hovered over Alicia.

"And this is our home for the next week," I said. "I can't decide for you whether to leave or not. That's up to each individual in this room. I'm sure George will be happy to arrange flights and transportation to the nearest airport for anyone who wants that. But I intend to stay. That's *my* individual decision."

No one said anything. Finally, Seth Hazlitt spoke up. "I agree with Jessica. I'm stayin', too."

"I'll get to work on a security plan right away," Mort said.

"Forget your security plan," Ken Sassi said. "I suggest we all try to put the murder out of our minds and get on with our vacation. This is a beautiful place, blessed by nature. I didn't bring all my fishing gear for nothing. Right, Jess? You and I have a date on a river."

I smiled. "We certainly do, Ken."

George asked, "Will anyone be leaving? If so, I'll start making travel arrangements straight away."

The only person who responded to George's offer was Jed Richardson, who said, "I'm sure you all agree that Alicia and I had a pretty big scare back in London. I'm over it, but I think Alicia here might not be." He looked down at her. "If you want to leave, honey, I'm with you."

She looked up with moist eyes and said, "No, Jed, I'd like to stay." To us: "We'll have a good time, won't we?"

"We sure will," Susan Shevlin said. "That's what we're here for."

"Let's eat," Mort said. "That salmon looks right good. Don't it, Seth?"

"*Ayuh*. That it does."

Forbes reappeared behind the bar, and we relaxed as we ate and drank.

"Where's Pete and Roberta?" Seth asked.

"In their room, I believe," George said. "They slept in this morning, and pretty much stayed there all day."

"They're missing the food," Mort said. "I'll go rouse them."

Realizing that Cabot Cove's radio station owner and his wife weren't there caused me to wonder where the other two couples were, the producer of horror films, Brock Peterman and his wife, Tammy, and Dr. Geoffrey Symington and his wife, Helen. I asked George.

"The doctor told me this morning that he was spending the day at the Wick Historical Society."

"Oh?"

" 'Research into something,' he said. "The Petermans disappeared all day, showed up a few minutes before your group came back from their tour. They and the Symingtons have paired up for dinner in town."

"Strange combination," I said.

"My thought exactly. Jessica, thank you for rallying your friends to stay. I would have hated to see them go. More important, I would have hated to see *you* go."

"I can't blame them for being concerned."

"Nor can I. Do you think your sheriff friend will actually concoct some sort of security plan, as he calls it?"

"Probably. Mort rises to every occasion, not always the right way but meaning well."

"*Rodden tree and reid threid.*"

I laughed. "And what does *that* mean?"

"Put the witches to their speed, Jessica. Sheriff Metzger might include in his security plan some amber beads and horseshoes, place some of each outside your bedroom doors each night. Supposed to be an effective deterrent to witches and warlocks."

"Should I suggest it to him?"

"No."

There were two hours before dinner, and everyone drifted to their bedrooms. George and I went to his office, where we'd met with Constable McKay earlier in the day. George offered me a glass of single-malt scotch, Old Pulteney, distilled and bottled in Wick. I declined.

"A pleasant brew," George said, pouring himself a small amount in a snifter bearing the Sutherland Clan crest. "After the events of the day, I rather think I'm entitled to it."

"You're entitled to it no matter what the events of the day have been."

"Thank you for that vote of encouragement, Jessica." He tasted the scotch, smacked his lips, and said, "Well, dear lady, what do you think now that you've had a day to ponder Daisy's murder?"

"What makes you think I've been pondering it?" I asked.

"Haven't you?"

"Of course I have. I'm being facetious. I think that even though reason should prevail, there is something terribly strange going on in Wick. I mentioned that we've had murders in Cabot Cove. Not many, but a few. The difference is—and I decided not to make the point with the others—the difference is that those murders didn't involve witchcraft, or allegations of it. No pitchforks in the chest. No crosses carved on throats. Just plain old run-of-the-mill murders. Jealousy. Greed. Ambition. A shot from a gun. The thrust of a kitchen knife. Poison in the tea."

"Or in the scotch?"

"Or in the scotch. The point is, there's never been anything mystical about murders in Cabot Cove, Maine. But this is so different, George. And as much as I dismiss as folly and overactive imaginations the notion of ghosts and witches, I must admit I've felt a certain chill up my spine since arriving at Sutherland Castle."

"The lady in white."

"Yes. And now this. George, can I ask you a direct question, one that might put you on the spot?"

"You know you can."

"Do you *personally* feel we're in any danger by staying here?"

He looked at me for what seemed a very long time, finished the scotch in his snifter, placed the empty glass on the desk, and sat up straight. "Jessica," he said, "if I thought you, or any of your friends were in danger, I'd have you on a bus for Inverness within the hour, and I'd sell this castle to the first person with a check."

When I didn't respond, he added, "Believe me?"

"Of course I believe you, George. Thank you for being direct with me."

"I intend to be direct at all times, Jessica. For

instance, I will not allow this week to pass without us having our day together—alone!"

"And let me be direct by saying that you can count on it. By the way, did you ever contact the gillie about a day on the trout stream for Ken and me?"

"As a matter of fact, I did. Rufus Innes is a fishing legend in these parts. Old, craggy, crusty, and irascible. But the best guide in Scotland. He'll take you out day after tomorrow, if that fits your schedule."

"I'm sure it does, but I'll check with Ken. Time for me to get ready for dinner. Thank you, George, for being so reassuring. Just having you around will give everyone a sense of safety and—"

The woman's scream reverberated off the castle walls, even pierced them to reach our ears. George leapt to his feet and out the door, with me in close pursuit.

We ran up the main staircase to find Charlene Sassi standing on the second-floor landing, her fist rammed into her mouth, her eyes wide with fright.

"Mrs. Sassi, what's happened?" George asked.

"I saw her," Charlene managed to say.

"Saw who?" I asked.

"That woman. The one dressed all in white. And—"

"And *what*?" George asked.

"There was blood on her chest. God, it was awful."

George and I looked at each other. And then Charlene fainted, going first to her knees, then pitching forward onto her face.

Chapter Ten

George and I helped Charlene to her feet, brought her into her room, and sat her in one of a pair of matching upholstered chairs by the window. George handed her a glass of water, which she eagerly drank.

"Feeling better?" I asked.

She nodded.

"Would you like me to call a doctor?" George asked.

"No. I'm all right. Sorry I passed out like that."

"You were shaken," I said.

"I sure was. Jess, could we—?" She looked at George.

"George, would you mind if Charlene and I had a few minutes alone?" I asked.

"Of course not. I'll be in the hall if you need anything."

As he opened the door, the voices of others who'd responded to Charlene's scream were heard. The closing door shut out questions they hurled at George.

"Can I get you something, Charlene?"

"No." She sat up and grabbed my arm. "Jess, you saw her, too, didn't you?"

"The woman in white? Yes. I mean, I thought I did. But I'm sure I didn't."

"Why do you say that?"

"I say that because I don't believe in ghosts."

"But I saw her, Jess. That means it—she—must be real."

"Charlene, ghosts aren't 'real.' "

"I know that. That's what's really scary. She wasn't real, yet she was. Who *is* she?"

"She *isn't*. What I mean is—well, George talks about her as being a descendant of the Scottish witch, Isabell Gowdie."

"Oh, my God."

"What?"

"*He* acknowledges her?"

"I don't think he really acknowledges her, Charlene. You don't know George as well as I do. Beneath that dour Scottish exterior is a kidder. I think he likes to talk about the woman in white because it gets a reaction."

"She's a descendant of that Scottish witch who was killed back in the sixteen hundreds, the one who had a pitchfork jammed in her chest, and a cross carved on her neck?"

"Charlene, I—"

"And another relation of hers was killed the same way twenty years ago? And Daisy—poor, pretty kid—Daisy gets it, too?"

"Why don't we forget about it for a few minutes, Charlene."

"Easy for you to say."

"No, it's not easy. It's just that when I *thought* I saw her, I reminded myself that there isn't any such thing as ghosts, and got over it."

Charlene removed her hand from my arm and turned away.

"Charlene, are you angry with me? Did I say something to offend you?"

She faced me again. "You sound so cold and callous, Jess. That's not like you. You make me out to be somebody who's acting foolish, who—what did you say?—who can't get over it like you did."

This time, it was my hand on her arm. "Charlene, I didn't mean anything by it. I was just trying to be helpful, and said the wrong thing in the process."

She managed a smile. "I know, Jess. You'd never be deliberately cruel. And you're right. I thought I saw her, that's all. I *thought* it."

"Do you know what George says?"

"What?"

"He says that if you tell someone to *not* think

of purple elephants, that's all they're able to think of."

"That's funny."

"Go ahead," I said. "I dare you to not think of pink alligators."

She shut her eyes tightly. "I won't," she said. "I will not think of pink alligators."

"What are you thinking of, Charlene?"

She opened her eyes. "Pink alligators."

We both giggled.

"Feeling better?" I asked.

"Much."

"Where's Ken?"

"He went outside to practice his casting."

"I should do the same. George has arranged for a guide for us day after tomorrow."

"Good. Ken'll love that. Go ahead, Jess, back to your room. I'm fine."

"Okay. See you at dinner?"

"Yup. No ghost takes away this gal's appetite."

As it turned out, Dr. Symington and his wife, Helen, joined us for dinner. When asked why they weren't dining in town with the Petermans, Helen Symington said only, "A most unpleasant sort. We prefer your company this evening."

By the time we'd gotten through another splendid meal prepared by Mrs. Gower, tension levels had diminished. We deliberately talked about everything other than Daisy Wemyss's brutal murder, evading the grim issue that would certainly have put a damper on the evening. We even joked once or twice about the lady in white. "She" came up over a dessert of chestnut cake with orange and cardamon sauce, and strong coffee, causing Dr. Symington, who as usual said little during dinner, to take center stage. He spoke slowly and deliberately in his clipped British accent, sounding very much as though lecturing a class of students.

"This alleged lady in white," he said, "and the reported sightings of her, clearly indicates an apparition of the first magnitude. The term apparition comes from three sources—the Middle English word *apparicioun*, the Old French term *apparition*, and the Late Latin *apparitio*."

"That may be true," Seth Hazlitt said. "But no matter what you care to term it, Doctor, two real live women have *seen* this apparition."

"They *think* they've seen her. We each have an inborn level of suggestibility. It is my assumption—no, allow me to be more specific—my close observation of the two women in question, Mrs. Fletcher and Mrs. Sassi, convinces me that they possess a heightened sense of suggestibility, perhaps a four on a scale of one to five."

"Excuse me for disagreein' with you," Mort Metzger said from the other end of the table, "but you don't know what you're talkin' about. Mrs.

Fletcher isn't suggestible at all. Not one bit. That's why she's so successful. She's a cool and collected woman who doesn't see things that aren't there, especially dead women dressed in white."

Dr. Symington listened patiently, his elbows on the table, his narrow chin cradled in his clasped hands. When Mort was finished defending my suggestibility level, Symington said in the same measured tones, "Perhaps you are right, Sheriff. You are a sheriff, are you not?"

"That's right. Cabot Cove, Maine, the U.S.A."

A thin, sardonic smile crossed over Dr. Symington's lips. "And as such, Sheriff Metzger, you are undoubtedly a student of human behavior, particularly aberrant behavior."

Mort frowned.

"Bad behavior," Seth Hazlitt said, helping.

"That's right," Mort said.

"And you've questioned many witnesses, I assume, who report to you what they claim to have seen at the scene of a crime."

"Of course. What are you gettin' at?"

"What I am getting at, Sheriff, is that many of those witnesses you've questioned have told you things they claim to have seen, yet really didn't."

"I don't know about that," Mort said.

"Sure you do," Peter Walters said in his deep, sonorous voice. "You're always complaining, Mort, about how witnesses can't be trusted to remember things accurately, even if they saw the event an hour ago."

"That's different," Mort countered. "Doesn't involve ghosts."

"But it's the same principle," Susan Shevlin said. "Don't you see that—?"

The debate went on for another half hour. I didn't participate content to take in the views of others at the table.

We'd no sooner retired to the drawing room for the ritualistic after-dinner drinks when Brock and Tammy Peterman arrived. He appeared to be agitated. He was perspiring, and spoke in a staccato rhythm. "Inspector Sutherland, I'd like to talk with you privately."

George, who'd been chatting with Ken Sassi about our upcoming fishing expedition, expressed his annoyance at being interrupted by scowling.

"Sorry to interrupt," Peterman said, "but you'll love this. Trust me, man. You—will—love—this!"

I wasn't completely successful in suppressing my smile at George's discomfort. But he played the proper host; he led Peterman from the drawing room, leaving behind Tammy, who looked bewildered. She and her husband were dressed in matching chartreuse jumpsuits of a crinkly material. Sneakers adorned his feet. She wore spike heels.

I went to her. "How was your dinner?" I asked.

"What? Oh, okay, I guess."

"Where did you eat? I might want to try it myself while we're here."

"I don't know the name. The food was greasy."

"Sorry to hear that. Your husband seems very excited about something."

She made a sour face, as though something distinctly unpleasant had been placed in her pretty mouth. I took it as a signal to pursue conversation elsewhere, and left her alone. She grasped the opportunity to depart the room.

Dr. Symington sought me out. "Mrs. Fletcher, I understand that not only did you see the castle's resident lady in white, she spoke to you."

"Oh, I don't think so. I mean, I *thought* I heard something. But then again, the birds outside were chirping away, and there was the wind. No, I don't think she said anything to me. In fact, I'm certain the entire episode was a figment of my imagination."

"I'm not certain that's true, Mrs. Fletcher."

"Oh?"

"I would like to conduct an experiment with you, if I may."

"An experiment? I don't think so. Is that why you're here, Dr. Symington? Doing research on ghosts?"

"Precisely. I've been aware of Sutherland Castle's reputation for being haunted for many years.

It took me this long to gather enough preliminary data to finally examine it in person."

"This castle is famous for being haunted?" I asked.

"No more so than dozens of others in the British Isles. But this area is unique, I feel, because a number of· its residents cling to the old ways and traditions, ancient myths and beliefs. Witchcraft, ghosts, warlocks, and the like seem to live on here, at least with a core group of people. That, coupled with the castle's reputation, provide someone like me with a fertile field of research."

"You mentioned an experiment you wanted to do with me. What is it?"

"You seem to be the sort of person who might attract this woman in white. Perhaps she feels you are someone who would be sympathetic to her."

"I don't understand," I said. "You called what I thought I saw to be an apparition. Now you speak of her as being real, someone who would find me a sympathetic character."

That tiny smile again. "Apparition? Real? That is the point, Mrs. Fletcher. One doesn't know with any certainty, does one? Perhaps we can find out. As a writer of murder mystery novels, I assume you have a heightened curiosity about such things."

"As a writer, yes. But not necessarily when it involves me personally."

George Sutherland and Brock Peterman reappeared.

"Where's Tammy?" the film producer asked.

"She went to your room," someone replied.

He left immediately.

"Got a moment?" George asked me.

"For you? Always."

"In the mood for some fresh air?"

"Sounds inviting."

We went outside to the castle's front courtyard. A dense fog had settled over everything. It was like standing in a cloud, an eerie feeling. I could see into the drawing room through a narrow window. Everyone inside was busy chatting; Roberta Walters's loud and distinctive laugh was heard. I smiled. These were my very good friends, and I was happy the latest intrusive events—Daisy Wemyss's murder, and Charlene's alleged sighting of the lady in white—hadn't put a permanent damper on their vacations.

"Come," George said, taking my hand and leading me across the grass and through the castle ground's main entrance. We crossed the road and stepped into a tiny park, with a bench and a small bridge crossing a narrow running stream.

"A pretty spot," I said. "I wish I could see more of it." The fog obscured everything beyond four feet.

"Tomorrow," George said. "When the fog lifts."

"What did Mr. Peterman want?" I asked.

"He wants me to pay for a camera crew to come here from Edinburgh, and put them up for a few days."

"Why?"

"He claims to have met someone in town who claims to be"—he laughed—"who claims to have all the answers to the murder of Isabell and Evelyn Gowdie, and poor Daisy."

"Do you think—?"

"No, I do not. This chap also told Peterman, at least according to him, that he knows the witches of Wick, and can arrange for Peterman to meet with them for filming purposes. For a price, of course."

"Of course. Will you pay for a camera crew?"

"No. Peterman is a volatile chap. Very angry that I declined to help him financially. Threatens to leave and use his next film to—how did he put it?—to 'trash' Sutherland Castle. On the telly."

"How dare he?"

"My sentiments exactly. I wish he and his wife would simply leave."

"Any chance of that?"

"We'll see. Are you all right?"

"Yes. Why do you ask?"

"All these abominable things happening since you arrived. Certainly, not what I intended your holiday to be."

"Someone once said, 'Life is what happens while you're making other plans.' I subscribe to that philosophy."

"The songwriter John Lennon."

"Is that who said it?"

"I believe so. How firmly do you believe in the sentiment behind those words, Jessica?"

"I don't know."

I realize—you've expressed it quite clearly to me—that your plans do not include another man in your life."

"I wouldn't say that, George. There are many men in my life."

"I don't mean men you simply know. Friends. I mean a man who might fill the same role your deceased husband, Frank, did so ably."

"Oh."

"I won't beat around the proverbial bush, Jessica. You know *I be keen o you.*"

I smiled. He'd said that to me before, and I liked the sound of it. "I know," I said. "And I'm fond of you, too, but in a different way than when Frank was alive."

"It's been a long time since you and Frank enjoyed life together," he said.

"A very long time."

"People shouldn't be alone for too long. Not good for them."

"I probably agree with you," I said. "But, in my

case, I don't need to be as close to a man as I was to Frank in order to feel I'm not alone. It's hard to explain, George. I have a wonderful life. I've been blessed. I had many years with a wonderful man, who unfortunately died much too soon. I've been blessed as a writer. I never dreamed when I started that my books would be best-sellers, and that I'd travel the globe to talk about them. I live in what I consider a heaven of sorts, Cabot Cove. I love it there, love the people, some of whom are with me on this trip. It's a close-knit community, each person caring about the other. With a few notable exceptions. Am I rambling?"

"No. Please go on. I have a feeling I'm about to hear the most elaborate explanation since meeting you of why my intentions are not to be realized."

"I wish you wouldn't put it that way," I said. "It makes me sad."

"Oh, no, no sadness, Jessica Fletcher, and I apologize for making you feel that way. I'm not a bloody schoolboy. I expect nothing from people except what they wish to give me."

"And I'm not a bloody schoolgirl," I said.

"Two graduates of life. You were saying?"

"I was saying that my life is idyllic. Full and fulfilling. I suppose if I were totally honest, I'd admit I am—"

"Yes?"

"I am afraid to change my life, George. It has nothing to do with any lack of feeling I have for you. To be truthful, I felt a spark the moment we met at Brown's Hotel in London. Remember?"

I saw his smile through the fog. "The spark singed me, too, Jessica."

"You questioned me regarding Marjorie Ainsworth's murder. I recall exactly what you wore that day. And I especially remember our parting on the sidewalk after tea, and watching you stride away."

"Hmmm."

Marjorie Ainsworth had been the world's reigning queen of mystery writers. I'd come to London to address a writer's group, and was Marjorie's weekend houseguest when someone stabbed her to death in her bed. The local authorities weren't up to the task of solving the crime, and Scotland Yard was called into the case. Enter Chief Inspector George Sutherland.

"Any other fond memories of our first meeting?" he asked.

"Just that as I went back to the Dorchester, I kept thinking about you. Of course, those pleasant thoughts were mixed with concern about some of the questions you'd asked me. I was a suspect, and I knew it."

"Only because you were there when Ms. Ainsworth was killed. *Everyone* was a suspect then."

"As it should be." I wrapped my arms about myself. "George, would you mind if we went back inside. I'm cold."

"Of course. Aren't you ever lonely, Jessica?"

"Honestly?"

"Nothing but."

"No. My problem is finding the time to do everything on my agenda. I'm always working on a book. There are so many things in the house to tend to. I have my garden. And I've become obsessed with the labeling machines someone gave me last Christmas. I'm labeling everything in the house. My friends joke that they're afraid I'll label them when they walk through the front door." I sighed and smiled. "No, George, I'm not at all lonely."

"I'm pleased to hear that, Jess. May I make an important announcement before we go inside?"

"Of course."

"You might not find it so important, but it's something I've had a need to say to you for quite a while."

"Yes?"

"I am in love with you!"

"But—"

"And *as ae door shuts anither opens.*"

"Translation?"

"We are never left entirely without hope." He took my hand. "Come. We can discuss it at another time."

Chapter Eleven

"Mrs. Fletcher, got a couple of minutes?"

Brock Peterman, dressed in a Hard Rock Café T-shirt, safari jacket, cargo shorts with numerous pockets, and alligator loafers, intercepted me on my way to breakfast the next morning.

"Yes?" I said. "What can I do for you?"

He motioned for me to follow him into a small room off the hallway. He was hyper, eyes darting every which way like tiny ball bearings in a fluid, his tongue working over his lips.

"You wanted to say?" I said.

"Yeah. Look, Mrs. Fletcher, I didn't know what a big star you were when we were introduced."

"Star? I'm not a star."

"Sure you are. Big-time murder mystery writer. Best-selling books everywhere. I don't read a lot. No time. That's why I didn't pick up on your name right away."

"You don't have to apologize, Mr. Peterman.

I've never seen any of your movies. I'd like to get to breakfast. You said you wanted to talk to me about something."

"Yeah. Look, you and I should pair up, you know what I'm saying? Here we are in this nut-house of a castle, this Looney-Tunes town called Wick. You and I can make one hell of a movie about this place and the murders. You write the screenplay, and I bring it to the big screen."

"Mr. Peterman, in the first place I don't write screenplays. In the second place, this lovely castle is owned by my dear friend, Inspector Sutherland. In the third place, I find Wick to be anything but Looney Tunes. It's a fine village, with good and decent people."

He guffawed. "Yeah, right. Fine, decent people who go around sticking pitchforks into girls' chests."

"Mr. Peterman, thank you for your kind words about me, and for the offer. But I'm not interested. I'm here enjoying a much-needed vacation and have no intention of collaborating with you."

"Wait a minute," he said. "I found this guy in the village who knows all about the craziness going on around here. I can introduce you to him. He'll give you enough material to write the screenplay, and a couple of books besides."

"Mr. Peterman, I—"

"We could do this with Sutherland, your

buddy. Maybe you can talk to him, convince him to bankroll a crew to come here. You promote your books. One of your friends says you travel all over promoting them. Promotion. That's the key to everything. I can help Sutherland turn this dreary dump into a real winner. He'd be turning tourists away."

I started to leave.

"Hey, Mrs. Fletcher, I'm talking megabucks. The silver screen. I can get this flick made if I have your name attached to it."

"Sorry, but you'll have to get 'this flick' made without me. Excuse me. I'm hungry."

The conversation with Peterman caused me to be the last one of my group at the breakfast table. Everyone seemed in good spirits, including Alicia Richardson and Charlene Sassi. We were served by Mrs. Gower and a new face, a tall young woman with large bright green eyes, flaming red hair, and an abundance of freckles splattered across her narrow face. Her name was Fiona, and her ready smile and pleasant voice were a delightful counterpoint to Mrs. Gower's stony and stern face.

"Where to today?" Seth Hazlitt asked as Fiona refilled our coffee cups.

"I haven't decided," I said. "Any suggestions?"

"Thought I might just stroll the village. Looks like a fat day comin' up. Sun should shine."

"Mind if I tag along, Seth?"

"Be my pleasure."

I turned to Mort Metzger: "You and Maureen interested in some serious walking?"

He asked his wife, who indicated she liked the idea.

"We'll go with you," Roberta Walters said.

"Us, too," said Susan Shevlin.

As we prepared to leave the castle to walk into Wick, Brock Peterman cornered me again. "Have any second thoughts, Mrs. Fletcher?"

"No. Well, let me ask you this, Mr. Peterman."

"Call me Brock."

"All right, Brock. I'd like to talk to this man in the village you say knows so much about local witchcraft."

He fixed me in an accusatory stare. "You wouldn't do an end run around me, would you?" he said, his tone indicating that's exactly what he thought I was doing.

"I don't make end runs around anyone, Mr. Peterman. Brock. But if you expect me to consider entering into a business relationship with you, you'll understand my need, and right, to see just how reliable your sources are."

"Yeah. Sure, I understand that." He pulled a slip of paper from the pocket of his safari jacket and handed it to me. The name written on it was *Evan Lochbuie.* "He comes off like a crazy old coot, but I think he's dumb like a fox. Runs a little boat from the docks, looks like a homeless bum—maybe he is—babbles on, drools a lot."

"Sounds charming."

"So you want to talk to him. Go ahead. You'll see why I'm hyped up over this flick. See you tonight."

"All set?" Mort asked when I joined him and the others in front of the castle.

"Yup. I have my walking shoes on, and my umbrella in my bag. Just in case."

"Have fun!"

We looked up at a window where George Sutherland stood, waving. *"Don't tyne the road,"* he yelled.

"What's that?" Mort shouted.

"Don't lose your way."

"Can't hardly do that," Mort replied. "You can see this castle from everywhere."

With that, we were off.

I ended up leading the pack, and decided to take a different route than I'd chosen during my first foray into Wick. It was a good choice; we were surrounded at every turn by natural beauty, walking at one point through a waist-high field of heather, looking down sheer black cliffs to the sea, waves crashing, hundreds of birds nesting in crevices or soaring into the sky that was, at once, menacing black and cobalt blue.

"Look over there," Roberta Walters, our resident bird-watching aficionado, said, training a small pair of binoculars at a small plateau atop a huge rock jutting up from the water. "A red-throated diver." She handed the binoculars to her husband, who confirmed the sighting while Roberta made a note in a bird book in which she listed every bird she'd ever seen.

We continued in the direction of town, looking back on occasion at Sutherland Castle, growing smaller as we distanced ourselves from it. But no matter how its visual dimensions decreased, its domination of the horizon continued to impress.

A golf course sat unused. Golf originated in Scotland, and the Scots's love of the game is legendary. But from the looks of this course, golf wasn't a popular sport with the citizens of Wick, or its surrounding villages and towns.

"Look at that," Mort said, pointing to something in the distance. "Looks like an oil rig."

" 'Course it is," Seth said. "Didn't you read your guidebook, Mort? There's oil all up and down Scotland's coast, includin' right there offshore from Wick."

Mort was offended at Seth's tone; they often slipped into such minor arguments that never progressed very far because of their long and deep friendship. Usually, I find their spats to be humorous. But on this day, I didn't want one to intrude into our pleasant excursion, and expressed my feelings.

"Just pointing out the obvious," Seth said.

"No need to put me down," said Mort, "just 'cause I missed the part about oil in the book."

"How can you miss it?" Seth said. "Everybody knows Scotland got rich 'cause a' oil."

"Doesn't look too rich to me around these parts," Mort countered.

"And it doesn't matter," I said, summoning steel into my tone. "Stop it!"

Seth and Mort looked sheepishly at me. Mort grinned. Seth shrugged. And we continued walking until reaching the beginning of Bridge Street.

"How about stopping in that shop," suggested Susan Shevlin. Its sign said it specialized in kilts and bagpipes. She'd been making notes ever since we left the castle. One thing is certain—Susan Shevlin is a hard-working travel agent, and her clients benefit from her conscientious approach whenever she travels.

The shop's inside was musty and dimly lighted. Behind the counter stood an older man with unruly white hair, red cheeks, and eyes sunk deep into his face. He was doing something with a bagpipe when we entered, looked up, nodded, and went back to his chore. We browsed kilt outfits on manikins that looked to have been crafted in another era. The clothing draped on them was dusty, like the shop owner.

"Why don't you buy one, Seth?" Roberta Walters suggested, laughing. "You have great legs."

"That might be true," he said, "but I'm not one to go around showin' them off."

"I don't think you have such great legs," Mort said, still stung by Seth's earlier comment about not knowing of Scotland's oil industry.

"How would you know?"

"Boys," I said.

"Sorry," they muttered.

I went to the counter, where the owner continued to do his work. "Excuse me," I said.

Another glance up, his hands still working.

"Fixing a bagpipe?" I asked.

"*Ay.*"

"Do they break often?"

"No."

"What happened with the one you're fixing?"

"Tenor drone. Cracked. Hole in the windbag."

"Oh. Is it hard to play a bagpipe?"

"*Ay.*"

"I've always wanted to try."

He stopped working and stood, placing large, gnarled, liver-spotted hands on the countertop. "You'd like to play the pipes?"

"Yes. I mean, I've always enjoyed hearing them

played and—well, I wonder if I have the breath to do it."

"Most people do. Care to try?"

I looked at the others, who were debating the way items of clothing went with each other on one of the manikins. Would I look foolish attempting to coax something resembling music from an unwieldy set of bagpipes? It occurred to me as I pondered this that I seldom not try something because of how I might look to others. The truth was that every time I saw the bagpipes being played, I harbored a secret little passion to try them.

"Yes," I said. "I'd love to try."

He motioned for me to join him behind the counter. Others noticed, and were soon bunched across the counter from where I stood with the owner.

"What are you about to do, Mrs. F.?" Mort Metzger asked.

"Seems plain to me she's about to play the bagpipes," said Seth Hazlitt.

"I know that," Mort said.

"Do you know how to play them?" Pete Walters asked.

"No. But I'm about to learn." I extended my hand to the shop owner and said, "I'm Jessica Fletcher. These are my friends. We're from

America, guests of Inspector George Sutherland at Sutherland Castle."

"Are you, now? You had a bit of bad news, didn't you?"

"Ms. Daisy Wemyss's murder? Yes, bad news indeed."

"There's evil forces about."

"An evil individual. That's for certain."

"More than that."

"Could you explain what you mean?"

"I thought you wanted to learn to play the pipes."

"Oh, I do. Sorry to have gotten sidetracked."

"Daisy was only a *bit* lassie."

"Bit? Oh, a young woman. Yes she was."

"Well, *it's aa by nou.*"

"Pardon?"

"It's over and done with. But it's not the end of it."

"Show me how to play the bagpipes."

"*Ay.*"

Focusing on the instrument caused him to become more talkative. He turned to the group and asked, "What did Nero play while Rome burned?"

Seth quickly answered: "The fiddle."

"Wrong," said the shop owner. "He played the bagpipe. Came from India first. Romans took it all over Europe. French liked it, too, played dance music on it. This is a Highland pipe. Biggest there is. Has a melodic range of a ninth."

"I knew that," said Mort.

"The hell you did," Seth said.

"Sure I did," Mort said. "Everybody knows Nero played the bagpipes while the city burned."

"Could I hold it?" I asked, indicating the instrument—and wanting to interrupt what was about to become another spat.

He handed me the bagpipes; I was surprised at how heavy they were.

"What do I do now?" I asked.

He positioned it in my arms, placing the windbag beneath my arm. "Quite simple, ma'am. You blow into this blowpipe and fill up the bag. Then you squeeze the bag with your arm against your body, only you have to keep blowing to keep the bag full. You play the melody chanter—that's the melody pipe—by using your fingers on the eight holes."

"Like this?"

I blew into the windpipe, and pressed the bag against my body. Nothing. I kept blowing and squeezing until suddenly an eerie drone erupted from one of the reeds at the end of a tube. I stopped blowing and looked at my friends, a smile crossing my face. "Pretty good, huh?"

They applauded.

The shop owner encouraged me to continue.

After a few more tries, I was actually able to create the characteristic droning sound of bagpipes, and to play what sounded to me like a wonderful melody over it. More applause. Even the shop owner patted his hands together.

"Well," I said, handing the instrument to him, "that was an experience. Fun."

"Would you be interested in buying it?" he asked.

"The bagpipes?"

"*Ay.*"

"Well, I don't know. I mean—buy a set of bagpipes? The last thing on my very long shopping list. Buy them? How much?"

He frowned, mumbled to himself, drumming the fingers of his right hand on the back of his left. "It's an old set a' pipes, ma'am, but in good repair. I've fixed 'em good. Like new."

"I'm sure you have."

Fifteen minutes later, I emerged from the shop carrying the bagpipes wrapped in a sheet provided by the shop owner.

"You can't walk around carryin' that," Seth said.

"You're right," I said.

I went back inside the shop and left the pipes with the owner, who sternly warned me that he closed promptly at four. I assured him I'd return well before that. I also asked him if he knew a fisherman named Evan Lochbuie.

"*Ay*. But why would a cultured woman like you want to talk to a *dug* like that?"

"Is he a dog?"

"The worst kind. Gives *dugs* a bad name to mention him in the same breath."

"What's wrong with him?"

"He's *daft*. A raving maniac, that's what he is."

"But I can find him at the dock?"

"*Ay*. But you do it at your peril."

"I'll take your warning seriously. Thank you."

"I can't believe you bought bagpipes," Jim Shevlin said when I joined them on the street.

"Should be fun to learn," I said.

"Maybe it's to impress your handsome Scottish inspector," Maureen Metzger said, giggling.

"Could be," Susan Shevlin added. "He can teach you how to play it."

"You may be my friends," I said pleasantly, "but you are incorrigible gossips. You should write soap operas."

"He obviously is smitten with you, Jess," Susan said. "You can see it every time he looks at you."

"We're good friends," I said. "Nothing more." His words the previous night as we stood outside the castle ran through my mind, as they had a dozen times since getting up that morning.

"Where to next?" Seth asked.

"Let's just stroll," I said.

"Where did you find Daisy's body?" Jim Shevlin asked.

"Up there." I pointed to the other end of Bridge Street. "But you don't want to see that. Hardly a tourist attraction."

"I want to see it," said Mort Metzger. "There's been a crime committed on my watch."

"On your watch?" We said it in unison.

"Absolutely," he said. "I may be on vacation, but I still have an obligation as a law enforcement officer to protect you as my friends and fellow citizens, no matter where we are in the world."

We looked at each other and suppressed smiles. We all love Mort Metzger, Cabot Cove's sheriff for many years, and a dear friend to all. He does tend to overstep his authority and responsibility at times, which only makes him even more lovable.

"Take us there, Jess?" Cabot Cove's new mayor, Jim Shevlin, said.

"If you insist."

We paused in front of the office building and read the plaque placed there by the Wick Historical Society: *"Site of the murder of Evelyn Gowdie, Feb. 11, 1976, descendant of famed Scottish witch, Isabell Gowdie."*

"Seems like a silly thing to commemorate." Jim Shevlin said.

"Witches seem to be popular here," Roberta Walters said.

"This where you found the body, Jess?" Mort asked.

"In back."

We walked down the dirt driveway to the litter-strewn yard behind the building. Wick's constable, Horace McKay, was standing where Daisy Wemyss's body had been. He wore wading boots, and held his very long fishing rod. A net hung from a ring on the back of his fishing vest. A creel was on the ground, at his feet.

"Good morning, Constable McKay," I said.

He nodded, but said nothing.

"I'm Jessica Fletcher. You might remember I discovered Ms. Wemyss's body."

"*Ay. I remember.*"

"These are my friends. We're all staying at Sutherland Castle."

"*Ay. I know that.*"

Silence.

"Well," I said, "I just wanted to show my friends where I discovered Ms. Wemyss's body. Going fishing, Constable?"

"*Ay.*"

"Good luck."

I led the group back to the street.

"Talkative chap, ain't he?" Mort Metzger said.

"Number'n a hake," Seth Hazlitt offered, invoking a Maine expression.

"Oh, no," I said. "He's not stupid, Seth. Just not a man with a lot to say."

We looked back up the dirt driveway to where Constable McKay stood watching us.

"Wouldn't want to cross that man," Seth Hazlitt said.

"And there's no need to," I said.

"Anyone feel like lunch?" Mort asked. "I'm mighty hungry."

There was a consensus that lunch was in order. I was the only one to demur.

"Sure?" Seth asked me. "That pub over there looks promising."

"Not hungry," I said. "Besides, I have someone I have to look up."

"That so? Who might that be?"

"A man named Lochbuie. Evan Lochbuie."

"What's he to you, Jessica?"

"Nothing. The producer, Peterman, told me Mr. Lochbuie knows all about witchcraft in Wick. Maybe I'll learn something from him to use in a book."

Seth looked at me skeptically. "Sure that's all on your mind, Jess?"

I smiled. "Enjoy lunch, Seth. I'll join you at the pub in less than an hour."

"Not really that hungry," he said. "Mind if I tag along to see this Lochbuie fella?"

"Of course not. I'm not even sure we'll find him. He supposedly hangs out on the docks. Operates a boat of some sort."

The others went to the pub, and Seth and I headed for Wick's harbor, only a few minutes' walk from Bridge Street. While Wick's "downtown" area was relatively deserted, the dock and harbor was a busy place. Dozens of ships and boats of every size and shape were docked, and men worked on them. A vessel with many years of wear on it had just arrived, and its cargo—vats of scallops—was being unloaded. A stiff breeze off the water was refreshing, the smell of fish adding to it a pungent tang.

"Know where this fella is?" Seth asked.

"No. We'd better ask."

Seth turned to the nearest person, a wizened older man repairing a net. "Excuse me, sir, but we're looking for Mr. Lochbuie." Seth turned to me: "Evan is it?" I nodded. "Mr. Evan Lochbuie."

The fisherman looked up from his task and grinned, exposing a set of large yellow teeth. "He'll be over there," he said, pointing to the opposite end of the dock. "Why would you want to see *him*?"

"My friend here wishes to speak with him."

The fisherman squinted at me, shook his head, and resumed his net mending.

We walked to where Evan Lochbuie smoked a curved pipe in his bobbing boat. "Mr. Lochbuie?" Seth asked from the dock.

He looked at his feet as though deciding whether he was, indeed, Evan Lochbuie. Then he slowly looked up, scowled, and asked, "And who might be looking for him?"

"I'm Dr. Seth Hazlitt. This is Ms. Jessica Fletcher."

"Doctor, you say. What kind of doctor?"

"General practice. I take it you are a fisherman."

"Among other things."

"Pretty village you have here," said Seth.

"Cursed village, you mean."

"Cursed?"

He laughed and drew deeply on his pipe.

While Seth and Even Lochbuie chatted, I took the opportunity to closely scrutinize the man Brock Peterman claimed had special knowledge not only of witchcraft in Wick, but of what had happened to Daisy Wemyss. He looked old, although I suspected he was younger than his appearance indicated. Like most men we passed on the dock, his face was weather-beaten, old shoe leather molded into plains and valleys, the skin sunburned to its depth. He was a small man with a large head on which a grease-stained baseball cap bearing the word "Yankees" sat at a jaunty angle. Although it was a relatively warm day, he wore a heavy black-and-red-plaid jacket over a tan shirt, overalls, and bulky brown boots.

"Got a minute?" Seth asked.

Again, a gaze at his boot tops before answering. "Might have. Depends."

"Depends upon what?" Seth asked, his annoyance level audibly rising.

"Depends on whether I want to or not."

"Let's go," Seth said to me.

"In a minute. Mr. Lochbuie, I'm a writer. Mystery stories. I might want to write a book about witches. No, actually, I'm considering writing a movie with someone you've met, Brock Peterman. He's a Hollywood producer."

Lochbuie nodded. "I've met him. Funny-looking fella."

"He tends to dress different," I said.

A cackle.

"Mr. Lochbuie, I understand from Mr. Peterman that you're the local expert on witches and witchcraft. Is that true?"

A nod.

"I've also been told that you know something about the murder of the young woman, Daisy Wemyss."

His head slowly went up and down.

"Well, since that's the case, would you share some of your knowledge with me?"

"Him, too?" Lochbuie said, nodding at Seth.

"Him, too."

"What do you want to know?"

"May we join you in your boat?"

"*Ay.*"

"Sure you want to, Jess?" Seth whispered.

"Absolutely. If you'd prefer to go back to the pub, I can—"

"And leave you alone with this nut? Not on your life."

Lochbuie's boat was about twenty feet long. It had a small forward cabin, behind which was the control console. Seth took my hand and helped me step down into it. He followed awkwardly, almost losing his balance. We sat in weathered wooden chairs facing our "host."

We stared at each other for what seemed an eternity. Finally, Lochbuie said after puffing on his pipe, "You're Sutherland's lady, aren't you?"

"I'm sorry."

"You're George Sutherland's lady."

"I'm afraid you have some bad information, Mr. Lochbuie. I am no one's 'lady'!"

His smile was crooked. "Not what I hear," he said.

"You heard wrong. Let's talk about witches, Wick-style," I said.

"Not without talking about Mr. George Sutherland."

"What does he have to do with witchcraft?"

"Everything. You want to know why strange things are afoot here in Wick? Look to the damn castle. Strange doings been going on here ever since it was built. Haunted, it is. Full a' ghosts. You ever see the lady in white who lives there?"

I looked at Seth. "Just imagination," he said.

"Is it now?" Lochbuie said. "And what about the Wemyss girl? Imagination?"

"What do you think?" I asked. "Do you know who killed her?"

"Fairly obvious."

"It is?"

"Can't have another witch growing up in Wick. Have to get rid of them if Wick is ever to get on its feet. They destroyed the herring fishing."

"Witches did that?"

" 'Course. Any fool knows that."

"I don't know that," I said. "I heard that your herring fishing industry fell on hard times because other countries came in with large ships and depleted the herring supply."

Lochbuie puffed, then said, "Once had more than a thousand ships catchin' herring from here. Biggest herring fishing port in the world."

"So I've heard," I said.

"Couldn't last, not with the curse of the damn castle Sutherland Clan built. Everybody knows that. Evelyn Gowdie got herself killed 'cause of the curse she put on the village. Daisy Wemyss, too. Caught the curse while working up there serving people, carried it down here like she had the plague. That's what it is, a plague."

Seth, who hadn't spoken since climbing into the boat, said, "You're talkin' a lot of damn nonsense. Know what we call people like you back home in Cabot Cove, Maine? We'd call you *some ugly*, ill-tempered old man spreadin' stories like this to get people all riled up."

I winced at the directness of Seth's words. Evan Lochbuie reacted to them, too. His face twisted into anger. He stood, stepped closer, and extended his finger at us. It was a long and misshapen finger, with a black fingernail at its tip. Now, as he spoke, his voice rose in pitch and was singsong:

> *"Rise up stick, and stand still stone,*
> *For King of England thou shalt be none,*
> *Thou and thy men hoar stones shall be*
> *And I myself an elden tree."*

"What in hell does *that* mean?" Seth asked.

"You will turn into stone!"

Seth stood. "What did you do, put some sort a' damn fool curse on us?"

Lochbuie cackled. "But you don't believe in curses."

"Bet your life we don't." He grabbed my hand. "Come on, Jess. Let's get away from this nut."

"And you shall live as stone for all eternity, unless—"

Seth had me on my feet now. Our movements caused the boat to dip and sway. Lochbuie said in an even higher-pitched voice, "Unless the pitchfork puts you out of your misery before spreading the Sutherland curse to others."

As he said it, he stepped even closer to me and jabbed his finger inches from my nose. "And with a cross carved into your heathen neck!"

Seth twisted to place himself between me and Lochbuie. As he did, he lost his balance. "Oh, oh, oh," he said, extending his arm in an attempt to right himself. But he couldn't do it. He went over the side with a loud splash into the harbor's black water.

"*Seth!*" I yelled. "Help him," I said to Lochbuie.

But all he did was laugh and turn in circles, his hands raised to the sky.

"Help!" I shouted to those on the dock. "Please, he'll drown."

Two burly young men extended a long boat hook to Seth. He grabbed it and was pulled to safety, his rescuers hauling him up onto the dock.

I climbed from the boat and went to Seth. "Are you all right?" I asked.

He spit water and shook it from his ears. "Look

at me," he gasped. "Soaking wet. Ruined my suit."

"Come. We'll get you back to the castle and into dry clothes." I looked around. "Is there a taxi?" I asked no one in particular.

"I'll take ye," a man said. "Got my automobile right over there."

As we headed for it, the rest of the Cabot Cove crew suddenly appeared on the dock. "What happened?" Jim Shevlin asked, looking strangely at Seth.

"An accident," I said. "Seth fell in."

"How?" Pete Walters asked.

"A long story," I said. "I have to get him back to the castle before he catches cold. See you there."

"Remember what I said!"

Everyone looked down into the boat where Evan Lochbuie was still ranting and raving about the curse he'd placed on us.

"Who the hell is *he*?" Jim Shevlin asked.

"A crazy old man," Seth said through chattering teeth. "That's all. Just a crazy old man." Then, without notice, he went to the edge of the dock, extended his finger at Lochbuie, and said, "You want curses, you old fool? I'll give you curses. May your bunions grow and your brain shrink."

He looked to me for approval. I smiled and nodded. "That's telling him," I said.

"I put him in his place good and proper. Come on, Jessica. The fella's waitin' with his car. And I need a brandy. Maybe even two. Wind's got me chilled to the bone."

Chapter Twelve

"I can't believe you did it, Jess."

"Why? It seemed a natural thing to do."

"Do you realize the difficulties you'll face?"

"Is it that hard?"

"So I'm told. I can't speak from personal experience, but I've known many pipers in my time. They all testify to the difficulty in learning to play the bagpipes."

I'd delivered Seth Hazlitt to his room for a warm bath and change of clothes. Now George Sutherland and I sat in his comfortable office discussing my purchase that morning. In the rush to get Seth back to the castle, I'd forgotten about having left the pipes at the shop where I'd bought them, but George dispatched Forbes to fetch them. They now sat on the floor next to me.

"Will you be giving a concert after dinner?" George asked, laughing.

"Heavens, no. I'm not even sure I want to try

and play them in the privacy of my room. The castle's walls may be thick, but—"

"I think you should play them to your heart's content. Now, tell me again about this unfortunate incident with Evan Lochbuie and Dr. Hazlitt."

"I didn't realize you knew Mr. Lochbuie, George."

"Everyone knows old Evan. Sort of the town character."

"A fair assessment. A little scary, too."

"How so?"

"When he started uttering his so-called curse at us, I found myself frightened. I didn't let on for Seth's sake, but it was there."

"A curse? Turn you to stone, will he? Old Evan really has gone off the deep end."

"Seems like it. I think I'll go up and check on Seth. I hope he doesn't catch cold. He shivered and shook all the way back to the castle. Lovely man drove us. After spending time with Mr. Lochbuie, I was beginning to wonder whether everyone in Wick was—well, was a little daft."

"I admit that same thought has crossed my mind on occasion, Jessica, especially when they're railing against the castle and the 'spell' it's supposed to have cast over Wick." He stood and extended his hands to me. I took them, and we faced each other. "Go check on your wet, cold friend. Practice these bagpipes until you're ready for your debut at Royal Albert Hall. I have some annoying paperwork to catch up on. See you at dinner?"

"Yes. Thanks for sending Forbes to get this."

George picked up the bagpipes and handed them to me. "Heavy."

"And unwieldy. See you later, George."

I took the bagpipes to my room, then knocked on Seth's door. He opened it wearing his robe over pajamas, and slippers.

"Feeling better?" I asked.

"Some. Still have the chills. Thought I'd take a nap before dinner."

"Sounds like a good idea. Want me to wake you?"

"*Ayuh.* Much appreciated."

He shut the door, leaving me concerned. Seth didn't look good. His face was an unhealthy gray. He'd been in his wet clothes for too long, and I hoped he wouldn't become ill.

I went to my room and gazed out the window. The sky was now overcast, and rain had begun to fall, whipped by the wind into that infamous horizontal rain pattern I'd been told about before coming to northern Scotland. It splattered off the windowpanes; trees bent, leaves flew. I saw a brilliant streak of lightning, heard the resulting boom of thunder. And then the room's lights went out, leaving me in virtual darkness.

I took candles from the fireplace mantel, lit

them, and placed them on a table by the window. Their glow was warm and comforting as the storm intensified. I considered going downstairs to see whether someone was trying to restore power to the castle, but knew my intrusion wouldn't help solve the problem. Power failures were undoubtedly a common occurrence at the castle, probably in the entire area. Back home, a simple call to the power company usually resulted in fast action, unless a storm was of sufficient proportions to kill power to thousands of homes. I somehow doubted whether that sort of service existed in Wick.

I picked up the bagpipes and was poised to exhale into the blowpipe when there was a knock at the door.

"Come in," I said.

The door opened, and the young man in kilts who'd given me his manuscript stood holding a flickering candle. I'd completely forgotten about his manuscript. It was on a table along with some magazines and guidebooks.

"Oh," I said. "Come in."

"Don't wish to disturb you, ma'am, but Mr. Sutherland asked me to check on your needs."

"I'm fine. Will the power be out long?"

"Hard to say. Happens all the time. Mr. Sutherland called the electric company. It's the storm. The castle's not the only one going without."

"I'm sure not. I must apologize for not having

147

read your manuscript. I started it but became distracted. I read the first chapter. It's quite good."

He looked disappointed.

"But I will get to it soon. Maybe tonight."

"You found the first chapter only quite good?"

"Yes. What I meant was it was—quite good, in my judgment."

His face brightened. "Sorry, ma'am. Here in Scotland, saying something is 'quite good' means it's only so-so."

"Oh. A problem of semantics. In America, when something is quite good, it's—quite good. Very good."

"I see. Sorry."

His eyes went to my bagpipes and opened wide. "Are those yours?" he asked.

I laughed. "Yes. I bought them today in town. I intend to learn to play them."

"I play the pipes."

"You do?"

"Oh, yes. My daddy taught me when I was very young."

"Would you teach me?"

"I'd be pleased, ma'am, provided Mr. Sutherland doesn't think it inappropriate."

"I'll talk to him. Will the power outage delay dinner?"

"I think not, ma'am. Mrs. Gower has a wood-stove to cook on, and we've ample candles."

"That's good to hear."

He continued to stand there as though having something else to say, perhaps on a difficult subject.

"Is there something else?"

"Yes, ma'am." He looked up and down the dark hall.

"Would you like to come in?"

He hesitated for a moment, then stepped into the room and closed the door behind him.

"Yes?" I said.

"Mrs. Fletcher, may I speak privately with you?"

"Of course."

"I mean, without it leaving this room."

"Absolutely."

"Well, it's about my girlfriend."

I didn't expect to hear that. If he was looking for some motherly advice from me, I wished he hadn't. I'm always uncomfortable being drawn into conversations about other people's personal dilemmas. But I'd opened the door, so to speak, so said, "I'm listening."

"I'm worried about her, Mrs. Fletcher."

"In what way? Her physical safety?"

"Exactly, ma'am."

"What causes you to think she might be in some sort of physical danger?"

He made a few false starts before blurting out, "This place, Mrs. Fletcher. It's Sutherland Castle that has me worried."

"Oh?" I wasn't sure I wanted to continue with this line of conversation, but didn't seem to have much of a choice. I invited him to go on.

"I thought I was doing the right thing by Fiona in asking Mrs. Gower if she could come to work here. Replace poor Daisy, you know."

"Fiona is your girlfriend?"

"*Ay.*"

"She's lovely. I met her at breakfast this morning for the first time."

"*Ay.* She's a fair lass. I'm smitten with her."

"As I can well understand. But why do you think she's in danger working here?"

"Oh, Mrs. Fletcher, you know what's been happening. Daisy Wemyss. The bloody woman in white prowling the hallways. This is a strange and forbidding place, Mrs. Fletcher. Cursed, they say."

"Now, wait a minute, Malcolm. It is Malcolm, isn't it?"

"*Ay.* Malcolm James."

"Well, Malcolm James, you don't really believe that this castle is cursed, do you?"

"I don't know what to believe, and that's the truth. I know one thing for certain."

"What's that?"

"Fiona's mother believes it. Yes, she does. And

she's blaming me for bringing her daughter up here to take Daisy's place. Vehement, she is."

"I don't think she has anything to worry about."

"My father, too, always talking about how Sutherland Castle ruined Wick."

"It seems the myth has become reality to a lot of people. Malcolm, you're a writer, and from what I read, you're a good one. Good writers don't fall victim to these sorts of outlandish rumors. Good writers evaluate what they see and experience with a clear eye and a reasoned response."

"I do that, Mrs. Fletcher. I do. But sometimes it's hard when everyone around you is filling you with such tales and beliefs."

"I imagine it is. What would you like me to do?"

"I was thinking you might be willing to talk to Fiona, maybe even talk to her mother. You're respected in the world as a writer. They'd listen to you."

"Talk to Fiona? Does *she* believe these rumors?"

"Oh, no. She thinks it's all funny, laughs about it all the time. But her mum is another matter. No giggles from her, for sure."

"Let me think about it, Malcolm. Maybe I can come up with something to help appease your—*will* Fiona's mother become your mother-in-law one day?"

"I pray for that, Mrs. Fletcher."

"I'll talk to you later."

"All right." He backed toward the door. "And about those bagpipe lessons. Anytime, Mrs. Fletcher. Anytime. Be my pleasure."

Power hadn't been restored when it was time to go downstairs for dinner. I carried one of the candles from my room, and shielding it with one hand, descended the staircase and walked into the drawing room, where others had gathered for cocktails. A dozen candles cast a warm golden glow over the handsome room. Forbes tended the bar, as usual, his face set in an unexpressive mask. Fiona passed a silver tray holding hors d'oeuvres. I could see why Malcolm was "smitten" with her. She was a beautiful, vivacious young woman, filled with life and possessing a bubbly laugh that lit up the otherwise shadowy room.

"How's Seth?" Jim Shevlin asked.

"I'm glad you mentioned him," I said. "I promised to wake him for dinner. Excuse me."

"I'll do it," Shevlin said. "I can use the exercise."

He left, and I plucked a few items from Fiona's tray. George Sutherland appeared at my side holding two glasses of white wine. "Sorry about the dimness," he said. "The folks at the power company say we might not have it restored until sometime tomorrow afternoon."

"We'll survive," I said. "Actually, the candle-light is—"

"Romantic? If so, I might suggest they drag their feet fixing the lines."

"I hope Seth is all right," I said. "Jim Shevlin went to wake him. I forgot."

"A good stiff brandy will fix him up, I suspect." He handed me one of the glasses, and we touched rims. "To a more pleasant stay," he said.

"That sounds good. By the way, Malcolm James stopped by my room."

"I know. I sent him."

"He's a nice young man. He gave me his manu-script to read."

"Manuscript. I didn't know he was a writer."

"He's written a novel based upon the murder of Evelyn Gowdie twenty years ago. I've read the first chapter. It's quite good." I laughed. "When I told him I thought it was quite good, he was disappointed. I didn't realize that saying 'quite good' means only so-so in Great Britain."

"Ah, yes, we speak the same language, yet we don't."

I looked to the door. "Jim hasn't come back," I said. "I think I'll go check on Seth."

"I'll go with you."

We bumped into Jim on our way upstairs. "I

was coming to get you, Jess," he said. "Seth is sick."

"I was afraid this would happen," I said.

Seth was in bed, the covers pulled up tight to his neck, his shaking visible beneath them. A single candle burned brightly on the night table.

I sat on the edge of the bed and touched his forehead. "You have a fever, Seth."

"*Ayuh.* I'm burning up."

"That crazy old man," I muttered, referring to Evan Lochbuie.

"My fault," said Seth. "Lost my balance, that's all. Should have known better."

"Well, be that as it may, you need a doctor."

"I'll fetch Dr. Symington," George said.

Seth sat up. "Keep that man away from me," he said. "He's no doctor, no matter what degrees he claims. He's a quack, researchin' into ghosts and that sort a' nonsense."

I looked up at George: "Can we call a doctor from town?"

"*Ay.* But the electrical outage might make it difficult to get one up here. I'll try."

George left the room, and I continued to sit with Seth. "Can I get you anything, Seth? A glass of water? Some brandy?"

"No. Can't believe I didn't pack medicines when we left home. Always do. Just plain forgot."

"It doesn't matter. George will have a good doctor here, and you'll be on your way to recovery."

The wind hadn't abated; an especially strong gust battered the window. "Like a real nor'easter," I said.

"That it is."

I could tell he was fighting to keep his eyes open, and decided the best thing was to let him rest until the doctor arrived. I patted his arm. "I'll be downstairs, Seth, but I'll check in often until George gets a doctor here. In the meantime, you rest."

"*Ayuh*, Jess. Thank you. You'd make a good nurse. Pleasin' bedside manner."

I no sooner had returned to the drawing room, where people were getting ready to go to dinner, when Jed Richardson, Cabot Cove's resident pilot, came into the room. "Has anyone seen Alicia?" he asked in a loud voice.

"Alicia?" I said. "No. Isn't she with you?"

"She was. About a half hour ago she said she was coming downstairs to check on the electrical failure. She never returned to the room."

"Probably got sidetracked with something," Charlene Sassi suggested. "Maybe ran across an interesting book."

"And read it in this light?" Alicia's husband said gruffly. "I'm worried."

George Sutherland, who was listening, said, "I

suggest we fan out and look for her. I'm sure she hasn't ventured outside, not in this blow." He assigned us to various areas of the castle, and we set out in search of her. As George and I were about to head out as a team, he looked to the bar: "Where's Forbes?" he asked aloud. "Always disappearing at the wrong time."

"Like Alicia," I said to myself.

We searched the area by his office, and rooms near it. "Where could she have gone?" I asked as we moved swiftly down a hall. As George was about to open a door to a storage closet, a man's voice from another recess of Sutherland Castle shouted, *"Help!"*

"That way," I said, leading us in the direction from which I thought the call had come. The man repeated his cry for aid, and we followed the voice until reaching its source—Forbes, the castle's jack-of-all-trades. With him was Dr. Symington, who bent over Alicia Richardson. She sat with her back against the wall behind a large suit of armor, its wicked-looking ax resting on the floor next to her.

"Alicia," I said, kneeling at Symington's side. "What happened?"

She shook her head and rubbed her eyes. I noticed a slight cut, and a widening green-and-black bruise on her left cheek.

I repeated my question.

"I don't know," she said. "I was walking here and—" She began to sob.

Dr. Symington helped her to her feet, and I steadied her until she was sufficiently recovered to stand alone.

I turned to Dr. Symington. "Did you find her?" I asked.

"Yes."

I looked for Forbes, but he was gone. "Was Forbes here when you found her, Doctor?"

"He arrived right after I called for help."

"*Right after?*" I said. "He must have been close by."

"I think we'd better get Mrs. Richardson to her room," George suggested.

"A good idea," I said. "Where's Jed?"

"Still looking for his wife," Symington said. "I'll go get him."

We settled Alicia on the bed in her room. Jed arrived and came to her side. "What in hell happened?" he asked.

"Looks like someone hit her," George replied.

"No," Alicia said, holding a towel filled with ice to her cheek. "I think I tripped."

"Over what?" George asked. "The ax?"

"Yes. Maybe. I just remember something hitting me in the face, and falling down. I grabbed at the suit of armor to keep from falling. Maybe I grabbed the ax."

George's expression said he didn't buy it.

"I'm just glad you weren't more seriously injured," I said.

Mort Metzger entered the room. "What's going on here?" he asked.

Jed Richardson filled him in.

"I should have put my security plan into effect," Mort said. He asked me, "How's Seth?"

"Sick."

I asked George about summoning a doctor from the village.

"I'll get to it straight away," he said. "Forgot to do it in the events of the evening. Dinner is ready. Provided, of course, you're still hungry after what has happened to Mrs. Richardson."

"No sense skipping dinner," said Mort.

"I'll check on Seth," I said.

"Mrs. Gower will send dinner to your room, Mrs. Richardson," George said.

"No need," Alicia said, dangling her legs off the bed and standing. "Just clumsy ol' me, tripping like that. I'd like to eat with the others."

Seth was asleep when I peeked into his room, and I didn't disturb him. As I walked into the dining room, George whispered in my ear that a doctor would be at the castle within the hour.

"That's good news," I said. "Funny, but I am hungry."

Fiona and Mrs. Gower served. I couldn't take

my eyes from Fiona after what Malcolm James had told me that afternoon. Was she really in some sort of physical danger? I didn't want to accept that, but considering what had already happened—Daisy Wemyss's murder in Wick, and Alicia's "accident" that evening, to say nothing of women in white floating about the castle—I certainly wasn't about to bet my house on it. Maybe Mort was right; we needed some sort of a security plan.

Alicia's fall had taken the edge off the group's usual ebullient dinner mood. There was conversation, of course, but it was markedly subdued compared to other evenings.

A simple dessert of sherbet and oatmeal cookies topped off the meal. By then, the mood had loosened a little, and Pete Walters began telling jokes. I remember laughing at the punch line of one, and enjoying the dialect he assumed for telling the second. But that's all I remember of it.

"Jess?"

I heard my name, but it didn't register.

"Jess? Are you all right?" It was George Sutherland's voice.

I heard the scrape of chairs, and was suddenly aware of people hovering about me. Someone placed hands on my shoulders and gently shook.

"*Gorry*," Mort Metzger said. "You look like a stone statue."

"What?"

I looked up into each person's face and eyes. "What's the matter?" I asked.

"You seemed to have fallen into a spontaneous trance," Dr. Symington said.

"Trance? Me?" I laughed. "Don't be silly."

"You sure looked strange," Susan Shevlin said.

"Like a stone statue," Mort repeated.

I looked to the head of the table, where George Sutherland sat. "Stone?" I said to him. "I looked like stone?"

"Easily explained, Mrs. Fletcher," said Dr. Symington. "You see, we are each capable of—"

"Stone," I muttered.

And the words of the crazy old man at the dock, Evan Lochbuie, filled my head, blotting out everything else being said.

Chapter Thirteen

The young physician summoned to Sutherland Castle, Dr. Hamish Dawson, was a pleasant young man, bursting with zeal for his professional calling. He examined Seth at length. When he was finished, he came downstairs and sat with George and me in George's office.

"No question about it," he said, "Dr. Hazlitt is ill. His fever is real. So are his shakes. But I can find nothing to cause it. All vital signs are strong. There's no hint of infection in his throat or ears. My suggestion is that we get him to the hospital in the morning and draw some blood, do other tests."

"Is that really necessary?" I asked. "It sounds to me like a good old-fashioned case of the flu." I added what Dr. Dawson was probably thinking: "Of course, I'm not a doctor."

"The man spent time in the water," George offered. "Got a chill from the air, was in his wet clothes for a period of time."

Dawson smiled. "I really don't think Dr. Hazlitt fell ill because of that," he said. "Shall I call the hospital and arrange to admit him in the morning? They're struggling because of the electrical problem, but the generators are working."

"Perhaps we'd better ask Dr. Hazlitt," George suggested.

"I will," I said. "Only be a minute."

As I anticipated, Seth wanted no part of any hospital. "A good night's sleep and I'll be fine," he told me. "Thank the nice young doctor for caring, but I'll do without his hospital."

I reported Seth's decision to Dr. Dawson and George.

"Fair enough," Dawson said. "After all, the patient is also a physician."

"I wonder if you'd examine Mrs. Fletcher while you're here," George said.

"Me?" I said, surprised. "I'm not sick."

The doctor looked at me. "Not feeling well, Mrs. Fletcher?"

"I feel fine. I wasn't the one who fell in the water."

"Jess," George said, his voice low and soothing. "We all saw what happened to you at dinner tonight. It wasn't natural. You went into a trance. Dr. Symington recognized it."

"A trance?" Dawson said.

"That's silly," I said. "I was—daydreaming, that's all."

"Looked like more than that to me," George said.

"Well, George, you're wrong. I've never felt better in my life."

"You looked as though you turned to stone, Jessica," George said.

I stood, went to a window overlooking a small garden, drew a deep breath, and said, "I can't believe you said that, George. 'Turned to stone,' indeed." I forced a laugh. "Maybe you'd better tell Dr. Dawson about the *curse* placed upon me."

Now Dr. Dawson stood. "Curse? Someone placed a curse on you, Mrs. Fletcher?"

"Supposedly." I told him in a mocking tone about the incident at the dock with Evan Lochbuie.

It was the doctor's turn to laugh. "Evan? Lochbuie? He's always putting curses on people. The man is certifiably insane. Belongs in an institution."

"Exactly," said George, coming to me and placing his large hands on my shoulders. "But you must admit, Jessica, that you did act strangely at dinner."

"All I did was to drift off into a sort of reverie. No, I don't need a doctor. But thank you anyway."

We walked Dr. Dawson to the front door. He'd

parked his small red sports car directly in front of the castle.

"Safe home, Hamish," George said.

"*Ay*, that I will, George. It was a pleasure meeting you, Mrs. Fletcher. Call again if your friend doesn't improve by morning. Hopefully, we'll have the power back on, and he'll be feeling tip-top."

"Thank you."

"And, Mrs. Fletcher, put Evan Lochbuie out of your mind. He's *hae a want*. Mentally defective, poor devil."

George and I watched him drive off, his head-lights piercing the gloom, now compounded by a dense fog that had settled over the coast.

Back inside, I asked George, "Why did you bring up my little dinner episode, George? I felt foolish having Dr. Dawson hear that."

"Because I care about you, Jessica. When I saw you at the table, I was worried. I don't know. Maybe having you and your friends here was a bad idea. All these unfortunate things happening to you. *I hae nae brou o this*, Jessica. I have no liking for what's been happening."

"I know that, George, but it's not your fault."

"Mrs. Richardson falling tonight and hurting herself. *I've never seen the like in aa my born days*. Bloody curses. Ladies in white with orange eyes. Young women killed with a pitchfork, like witches in olden days. I'm sorry I asked you here under these circumstances, Jess. I always wanted you to visit and share this place with me. Please accept my apology."

"And I've told you that no apologies are necessary. Tell you what. Let's consider everything that's happened to be far in the past. In the morning, we'll start our *real* vacation at Sutherland Castle. Ken Sassi and I have a lovely day of fishing planned. What's the gillie's name?"

"Rufus Innes. The best fishing guide in northern Scotland. A little eccentric but—"

"Another eccentric?"

"Pleasantly so. You were saying?"

"I was saying that tomorrow begins our official vacation. No more ghosts or curses or accidents. Just fun. A day on the stream for Ken and me. Tours of this spectacular countryside for others. Good wine and food, and good conversation. The way it should be."

George nodded and smiled. "Is the glass always half full for Jessica Fletcher? Never half empty?"

"Oh, it empties from time to time, George. When I allow it to. But I don't intend to allow it to for the duration of my stay in Wick."

"You lift my spirits," he said.

"Exactly what I meant to do. Now, let's join the others. They said they were going to play charades. Should be fun. Ever play?"

"No."

"Well, you're about to. I suspect you'll be very good at it."

I was right. George threw himself into the game, and after getting over his initial reserve and stiffness, helped the team led by Roberta Walters to victory. I was on Susan Shevlin's team, which also included Mort and Maureen Metzger. Mort is a better sheriff than charade player, much to his wife's overt chagrin; they fought for most of the game.

The film producer, Brock Peterman, and his wife, Tammy, declined to participate, as did Dr. and Mrs. Symington. Peterman took me aside before we started playing to ask whether I'd met up with Evan Lochbuie.

"I certainly did," I said.

"What do you think?"

"To use an old Scottish expression, I think he's *hae a want.*"

"What's that?"

"Crazy! I'll pass on your movie idea."

"Suit yourself. But you're missing out on a megaproject. Megabucks."

"I'll just have to live with it. Excuse me. Charades awaits."

I found myself yawning by the time ten o'clock rolled around. I wasn't alone. Others also seemed ready to call it a night.

"A quiet brandy or sherry, Jessica?" George asked.

"Afraid not. This lady is tired. And as you know, the fishing's always better early in the morning. You said the gillie would meet us here at five?"

"*Ay*. And ol' Rufus is prompt."

"So are we. Enjoy charades? You played well."

"Quite a lot of fun. We must do it again."

"I agree. Good night, George. I'll peek in on Seth before I go to bed."

"All right. I was thinking that the day after tomorrow might be a good day for us to get away together—alone. A private tour, lunch in my favorite pub, a relaxing time. The weather forecast is favorable, and I'll have caught up on my paperwork. Good with you?"

"Good with me. Good night, George. Thanks for everything." I kissed him on the cheek and went upstairs.

I tiptoed into Seth's room and stood at the side of his bed. For a moment, I wondered whether he was alive. He was on his back, and his breathing was barely discernible. I leaned closer. His shaking had stopped, but his usually pleasant round face was fixed in a stern, severe expression, mouth turned down at the corners, eyes squeezed tightly shut. He looked to me like—like a statue.

A *stone* statue.

I quickly left his room and went to mine, where I sat at the window staring into the darkness. The wind moved the fog in angry swirls, creating grotesque shapes that came and went, suddenly attacking me, then twisting away to be replaced by another burst.

I drew the drapes, prepared for bed, and lay awake for a very long time. My mind was filled with unpleasant images, which I fought to dispel. I was finally able to do that by focusing on the next day's fishing with Ken Sassi and our Scottish guide. That contemplation is always so pleasant for me that I was eventually able to close my eyes and drift off.

Unfortunately, it was not a peaceful, regenerating sleep. I awoke at four to my travel alarm's tiny bell, feeling as though I'd been drugged. I forced myself from the bed and went to the bathroom, where my mirror image projected a very tired woman.

Maybe George was right.

This had not turned into the pleasant and relaxing vacation I'd hoped for.

Chapter Fourteen

George had arranged for Forbes to cook us breakfast before setting out with our gillie—our fishing guide—Mr. Rufus Innes. Our host joined us at the ungodly hour of four-thirty as we enjoyed pancakes, bacon, and steaming hot coffee under the flickering glow of candles. To my surprise, Seth Hazlitt showed up, too.

"What are you doing up?" I asked.

"All slept out," he replied.

"But how are you feeling?"

"Tip-top, Jessica. That's all I needed, a good night's sleep. I'm rarin' to go."

"That's wonderful," I said. "But don't overdo it."

"Listen to her," Seth said with a chuckle. "You'd think she was the doctor."

After Seth returned to his room, and armed with a thermos of coffee for each of us and picnic lunches in wicker baskets, Ken Sassi and I went with George to the front of the castle, where Mr. Innes sat waiting in a battered Ford truck.

"Rufus, meet Jessica Fletcher and Ken Sassi."

Innes got out of the truck and extended his hand to me, then to Ken. He was short and chubby, with red cheeks and bright blue eyes. I was surprised at his lack of stature. For some reason, I expected Scottish fishing guides to be big, gruff, raw-boned men.

Back in Maine, our guides often display a certain disdain for those they guide, viewing them as necessary evils from whom they earn a living during the fishing season. To hear their tales could lead one to share that cynicism. Inexperienced, demanding, too often wealthy people who decide to take a fling at fly-fishing, look down on their guides as servants. In those cases, the guides get through it with clenched teeth and forced smiles until the day on the stream ends, and they can swap stories with fellow guides about the "sports" they put up with, an unflattering term in Maine for fishing clients.

"A pleasure to make your acquaintance," Mr. Innes said. He wore tan lace-up boots, heavy tan pants I assumed were lined, a dark green cable-knit sweater, and a black windbreaker that had been through many fishing seasons.

"We're so happy to have you guide us," I said.

"George says you know where the big ones are waiting."

Innes laughed. "If I could be sure of that, Mrs. Fletcher, I'd be a rich man. Might even own a castle myself."

"You're lucky you don't," George said. "Better off being a gillie."

"See you at dinner," I said.

"Many thanks for setting this up," Ken Sassi said.

"Fish good. And stay away from rabbits," said George.

"What?" Ken and I said in unison.

"Rufus will explain. Have a splendid day."

We loaded our gear in the back of the truck, and squeezed in the cab with Mr. Innes. There was a distinct chill in the air at that early hour, a harbinger of what was forecast to be a crisp, clear, and sunny day, perfect fishing weather unless you subscribe to the belief that fish rise more readily under overcast skies. I don't.

We bounced along over rutted roads, passing through dense forests, saying little to each other except the occasional comment about the gradually emerging sunrise, birds winging from tree to tree, and the fine day it promised to be.

Ken eventually brought up what George had said about "rabbits."

Innes laughed. "Old superstition among fishermen in these parts," he said. "Have a rabbit come near you when getting set to go out for a day of herring fishing, you'll have terrible luck. Anybody even mentions rabbits near fishermen puts a curse on them."

Another curse. Wick's most popular pastime.

By the time we reached a one-lane dirt road that ran past widely spaced farmhouses, the sun was fully up, working to burn away the last wisps of ground fog. Innes pulled onto a strip of grass and shut off the engine.

Ken got out and looked around. "Where's the stream?" he asked.

"Over there," Innes said, pointing to a meadow beyond the closest house.

"How do we get to it?" I asked, not seeing any path from the road to where Innes had pointed.

"Walk" was his answer.

Ken and I retrieved our gear from the truck and followed our guide, who started out across the property on which the house was situated. I was uncomfortable walking there, feeling like a trespasser. Maybe our guide had some sort of arrangement with the farm's owner. I asked.

"Oh, no, Mrs. Fletcher. No need for that. It's understood that any fisherman can cross anybody's property to get to a stream, as long as we close gates and don't destroy nothing."

"That's certainly an enlightened view," I said.

"Not like back home," Ken Sassi said.

"No, it's not," I said, continuing to keep pace with Ken and our gillie.

We crossed a large cow pasture, climbed a couple of low fences, passed through a decaying wooden gate, and eventually reached the fishing stream, fifty feet wide and fast-flowing.

"We'll start you out here," Innes said. "Should be some nice hungry brown trout in these parts."

Ken and I went through the ritual of putting on our equipment—multi-pocketed vest, chest-high Neoprene wading stockings held up with suspenders, over which we put our felt-sole lace-up wading boots. We attached each other's nets to rings on the back of the vests, secured wading belts about our waists to keep water from gushing into the waders in the event of a fall, and hooked fold-up wading staffs to the belts.

As we went through these preliminaries, I saw Mr. Innes watching us closely, a bemused smile on his face.

"Like going to war," I said lightly.

"*Ay.* The way *you* do it."

"What's wrong with the way we do it?" Ken asked.

"Nothing. Except it takes a lot of work, doesn't it?"

"Ready?" Ken asked me, ignoring Innes's comment.

"All set."

Rufus Innes had brought with him a fishing rod as long as the one I'd seen Constable McKay carry. "Mind if I fish, too?" he asked.

"Not at all," Ken said.

"What works in this river?" I asked, referring to the type of artificial fly to use.

"I like emergers this time of year," he said. "Hare's ear. Ants work pretty good, 'specially if you cast 'em under overhanging trees. Might try a streamer, too."

I chose a pretty little hare's ear emerger, which I attached to my hook, pleased I hadn't forgotten how to tie the required knot. Ken went with a long, brightly colored streamer. We used our wading staffs to check the floor of the stream, and carefully entered it. I loved the feel of cold water against my ankles, calves, and finally hips as I waded to where I felt comfortable. Ken did the same twenty yards upstream.

I turned to see what Rufus Innes was doing. He stood on the bank using his long rod to cast across the stream, almost reaching the opposite shore, which we could do only by being halfway across it. I now knew what he meant when he gently criticized our approach to fishing. For him, no waders, no boots, no cumbersome equipment. Just stand on the bank and cast.

I put the differences between our fishing styles

out of mind and began to cast, pleased with how after not having done it for quite a while I was able to lay my tiny artificial fly where I wanted it, in a swift channel running beneath an overhanging tree that would provide what trout like: shaded cover. I'd been at it for ten minutes when I saw Rufus hook a fish and skillfully bring it to shore. He lifted the plump sea trout from the water with his hand and examined it, lowered it back into the water, moved it back and forth to force water into its gills, and sent it on its way.

I resumed casting.

A half hour later, Innes had hooked and released two additional trout; Ken and I hadn't had as much as a rise.

"Want to move on?" our guide asked from the bank.

I looked to Ken, who nodded. We waded out of the stream and stood next to Innes.

"You did pretty good," Ken said to Innes.

"A little luck. I'll take you to a special place where I know you'll catch fish. Wouldn't want to return you to George Sutherland without a few fat trout in your creel."

We got back in the truck and headed west, I think, until entering a low range of hills that gradually rose in elevation until we were granted a stunning view of Wick, the surrounding countryside and coastline, and Sutherland Castle standing lonely and forbidding. Innes stopped to allow us to drink in the view.

"It's so beautiful," I said.

"Of God's making," Innes said.

"Is there a stream up here?" Ken asked.

"Oh, yes, there certainly is. A gem. I don't take many clients up here. None of the guides do. We try to keep it to ourselves."

"That sounds wise," I said.

"But for two a' George's guests, I'll make an exception."

"Much appreciated," Ken said. "Where's this stream? Looks like we might get rained out before long."

We looked up into what had been a pristine blue sky, with more of the same in the forecast. An ominous line of black clouds, twisting thousands of feet into the air, approached from the west.

"Weather here is changeable," said Innes. "Very changeable."

"So we've noticed," Ken said.

After another fifteen minutes of driving along a road so narrow the bushes on both sides scraped the truck, we came to the bank of a raging river about twenty feet wide, cascading down from the hills and picking up speed as it roared through the brush-laden gully in which we stood. The wind had now picked up; sudden gusts sent my hair flying.

"Running pretty fast," Ken observed. "Tough wading."

"Maybe we can do what Mr. Innes does, Ken, fish from the bank."

"No," Ken said, getting ready to enter the stream. "See that pool? I can smell fish in there."

"Might be," Innes said, "but too far to reach from here in this wind."

"Game?" Ken asked me.

"Sure," I said.

Ken entered the fast-moving water. As I was about to join him, the guide suggested I fish farther upstream. "Might be easier wading there," he said. "I've pulled some nice fish from that pool."

I took his professional advice and followed the riverbank upstream to what appeared to be a gentler access to the water. As I walked, I took in my surroundings. Despite the now-overcast skies and the wind, which seemed to increase in velocity with each step, I was supremely happy. The world had disappeared, as it always did for me when I was in, or near, a fishing stream. It would be nice to land a trout or two, but it certainly wasn't necessary to assure my continued happiness. Just being there was enough.

I'd almost reached the spot I'd selected to enter the stream when I noticed a wooden bridge spanning the river. I hadn't seen it before because its weathered wood had turned ash gray, melding into a pewter sky.

I'd learned years ago that the water beneath bridges was often a prime spot for fish to congregate. I looked back; Ken was waist deep in the water and casting to the pool. I smiled; this was his favorite way to spend a day despite working as a Maine guide for others. If Ken Sassi were a shoemaker, he'd be making shoes for his children on his day off.

I reached my spot and surveyed the water. I'd made a good choice. The riverbed sloped gradually into the deeper water, which would allow me to get farther out, hopefully within casting distance of a dark pool of water that spread from the shadow beneath the bridge into more open water.

I had one initial reservation about stepping into the river. Good fishing sense dictates that you should always fish in pairs when in a strange stream, especially when conditions for wading are less than ideal. I would have preferred to be closer to Ken and the gillie, but the lure of that spot under the bridge, and the promise of the fish it held, were too compelling. I'd be careful, each step taken with care, my wading staff helping me remain upright, my eyes focused on the riverbed in search of rocks, or falloffs into which I might misstep.

I entered the river and slowly, methodically headed for where I wanted to cast. The force of the water was stronger than I'd anticipated from the shore. Still, with my wading staff used to aid in counteracting the flow, I felt confident and secure.

I reached the spot and made sure my wading boots were solidly planted in the silty soil. I tossed my hare's ear fly into the water, increasing the length of my cast with each forward motion of my arm. But at its maximum length, I fell short of my target, the relatively still water under the bridge.

What to do?

A rising trout caught my eye, breaking the water to gulp down an insect, leaving telltale circles on the surface. There was another fish rising. And another. A hatch of insects had formed on the river. I looked to my immediate left and right and saw what they were. They weren't identical to my hare's ear fly, but close enough to fool a few trout. The trick was to get closer to the feeding fish.

Because the water was incredibly clear, I could see the ground beneath it. There appeared to be a path of sorts leading between large, slippery rocks to the pool under the bridge. If I took my time and stepped with care, I could bring myself within striking distance of the hungry fish.

I looked back to where Ken was still in the water, Rufus on the bank observing him. They looked very small in the distance.

I moved toward my next vantage point. I'd chosen a good path; I had little trouble navigating the current to get to where I wanted to be. I reached it and looked up. I was within twenty feet of the bridge, close enough to cast into the pool.

I applied some floatant to my fly to help it stay on the surface of the water, and started to cast. I felt good, my back cast straightening out behind me in textbook fashion, then coming up and forward in a straight line despite the wind, the fly on the edge of the hair-thin tippet landing gently where I wanted it to.

"Pow!"

A fish broke the surface and clamped onto my fly and the hook. The line straightened out and started to run from the reel as the fish sought the freedom of more open water. I gave him plenty of line. Judging from the pull he exerted, it was a good-size fish, with plenty of energy and fight. I didn't want to play him too long and exhaust him. Better to reel him in as soon as possible, and release him before he was dangerously tuckered out.

I started to bring in line with my right hand, my left holding the bending rod and catching the loops of line as I gathered them. My entire focus was on this task, a liberating experience. I was so devoted to properly and effectively bringing in this fish that I never really saw the man who suddenly appeared on the bridge. I mean, I saw him, but only for a split second, just long enough to see a six-foot-long log, about six inches thick, come hurtling down at me from the bridge. I gasped, and twisted to avoid being hit by it. I was successful, but in the process I lost my footing. Simultaneously, the rod slipped from my hand. I didn't know what was more important to me at that moment, keeping myself upright, or losing the rod, my favorite, given me as a birthday gift many years ago by my deceased husband, Frank.

There really wasn't a choice to be made. I was powerless on both counts. The rod disappeared, and I tumbled into the water. My head went under, but I forced it to the surface, spitting water all the way. The current grabbed me and headed me downstream, in the direction of Ken Sassi and Rufus Innes. I felt my waders begin to fill with water despite the belt around my waist.

I fought against being swept away; I'd noticed a particularly deep section of the river between where I'd fallen and where the others were. My mind raced. If I reached that deeper area and my waders filled, I'd be dragged down for certain. Thoughts bombarded me.

How many fly fishermen die in drowning accidents each year? A hundred? Two hundred?

Where was my prized fishing rod? Would I ever see it again? Would I be alive to use it again?

The water in my waders was sinking me fast. I grasped for rocks to keep from sliding down the river, but my fingers kept slipping from them, bruising my knuckles and elbows. My face hit a rock, sending a sharp pain from my cheekbone to my brain. I continued to fight to keep my head above water, but knew I was losing the battle.

I tried to call for help; each time I did, water gurgled into my open mouth.

What will they say in my obituary?

Will I be missed back home in Cabot Cove?

I'll never see George Sutherland again! So much to have said, so much to say.

I reached the deep center of the river, and started to sink. I flailed my arms, and managed a cry for help. I didn't know whether anyone heard me. I closed my eyes and resigned myself to dying in this beautiful river in northern Scotland.

Then strong hands grabbed me. I opened my eyes to see a blurry Ken Sassi wrapping his arm around my neck. Would he try to save me as lifeguards do, swim with me in-tow to the shore? A long, slender stick appeared above the water. A fishing rod. Ken grabbed it, and we were pulled from the deep pocket to shallower water nearer the shore. Now I could see Rufus Innes hauling us in on the end of his fishing rod.

Ken helped me to my feet. We were still in the river, but the water reached only my waist.

"I fell," I said, shaking water from my face and hair.

"I didn't think we'd make it," he said. "Damn, good thing I looked for you. Wanted to see if you were having any luck. Bad luck, I'd say."

"Yes."

"Lose your footing?"

"Yes. I—"

"Come on out of there," Innes yelled from shore.

"Good idea," I said.

We walked to the shore. For me, *waddled* is more accurate. My waders were like water balloons, making walking almost impossible. The minute we were on solid ground, I steadied myself on Ken as I slipped my suspenders off my shoulders, undid the belt, and slid down the waders, the water splashing all around me. I sat, removed my wading boots and the stocking waders, and breathed multiple sighs of relief.

"Treacherous out there," Innes said matter-of-factly.

"What happened, Jess?" Ken asked.

"I hooked a fish and was fighting him when—"

"When what?"

"When—when someone threw something at me from that small bridge."

"Threw something at you?" Mr. Innes said.

"Yes."

"Why would anybody throw something at you?"

"I don't know. To cause me to fall? To knock me down? To *kill* me?"

Chapter Fifteen

I wanted to continue fishing, albeit in calmer surroundings. But Ken and Rufus Innes wouldn't hear of it. I didn't argue too strenuously because I was soaked to the skin, and cold.

We returned to Sutherland Castle, where George was snipping flowers in the front garden for that evening's dinner table. Dr. and Mrs. Symington played croquet at one end of the lawn, while Jed and Alicia Richardson batted a badminton shuttlecock to each other across an imaginary net.

"What happened to you?" George asked when I got out of the truck.

"I fell in the stream."

He laughed.

"I'd laugh, too," I said, "if the reason for falling weren't so upsetting."

His mood immediately turned sober. "Why did you fall?" he asked.

Jed and Alicia joined us. I replied to George,

"Let me get out of these wet clothes and into something warm. I'll tell you then."

As I walked to the castle's front door, I heard Ken Sassi say, "She claims somebody threw a log at her from a bridge above where she was fishing."

And I heard George say, "Another incident. Excuse me. I have a call to make."

An hour later, I sat in the room with the huge fireplace where I'd first met Malcolm James, the young helper who'd given me his manuscript. A roaring fire sent warmth into the room; I reveled in it now that I was in dry clothes. A steaming cup of tea cradled in both hands enhanced the feeling. The electrical power had returned to the castle, which was welcome news.

With me were George Sutherland, Ken Sassi (his wife, Charlene, was off on an excursion into Wick), Jed and Alicia Richardson, Dr. Symington and his wife, Helen, our fishing guide, Rufus Innes, and Constable Horace McKay, who'd been summoned by George. I'd told my story of having fallen into the river, and how a log thrown at me from the bridge had caused it.

"You didn't get a good look at the chap who threw it?" McKay asked.

"No. Just a fleeting glance."

The constable frowned and grunted. Dr. Symington, who'd said nothing as I recounted what had happened, now leaned forward in his chair. "Mrs. Fletcher, are you certain you saw someone on the bridge?" he asked.

"Yes."

"But only a 'fleeting glance,' as you put it."

"That's right. A figure. Just for a moment."

"Like the lady in white?" he asked. He had the annoying habit of raising his voice at the end of every sentence, whether he was asking a question or not.

"You aren't suggesting that it was my imagination."

"Oh, no, Mrs. Fletcher. But in my many years of research, these sort of—how shall I put it?—these sort of sightings often have a tangible explanation, generally having to do with light refraction and other natural phenomena that cause us to think we've seen something real that doesn't actually exist."

I kept my annoyance in check as I said, "I'm sure your research is valid and useful, Dr. Symington. But in this case, there was someone on that bridge who threw the log at me."

"Did either of you see anyone throw the log?" Constable McKay asked Ken and Rufus.

They shook their heads.

"Did you see the log come floating by?"

"No," Ken said. "We were too busy trying to save Jessica from drowning."

McKay stood and stretched. "Well, I suppose I might as well go up there and take a look around. Won't find anything, I'm sure, but it's my job."

"While you're there," I said, "you might look for my rod. I lost it when I fell. It has sentimental value for me. My late husband gave it to me as a birthday gift."

"Bamboo?" McKay asked.

"No. Fiberglass, an early model."

"I'll keep my eyes open for it. Might have washed up on shore."

"Think I'll come with you, Horace," Rufus Innes said. "Two sets of eyes might be better 'an one."

George showed them out. When he returned, he said, "I considered joining them."

"I'd like to go back," I said.

"Me, too," said Ken.

"May I accompany you?" Dr. Symington asked.

"Why not?" George said.

"Do you know the spot?" I asked.

"*Ay*. I've done my share of fishing there."

"I thought you didn't fish," I said.

"Not any longer. But I did as a youth. You can't grow up in Scotland and not fish. Then you become older and find better things to do."

"Like what?" Ken asked.

"Catching criminals. Come."

As we left the castle and walked to the minibus

parked outside, Mort and Maureen Metzger and Seth Hazlitt arrived in a car driven by Forbes. "Where are you headed?" Mort asked.

"A fishing stream," I said.

"Wearin' that?" he said, referring to my sweat-suit and sneakers.

"I fell in earlier," I said.

"How did you do that?"

"It was easy," I said. "We're going back to try and find my rod. I lost it when I fell."

"We'll come help," Seth said.

"I suggest we get going," George said, a trace of pique in his voice.

We all climbed into the bus, except for Maureen Metzger, who said she preferred to stay at the castle. Having Dr. Symington with us set me a little on edge. There was something about the man that was off-putting. Of course, I had to admit he'd angered me by questioning whether I'd actually seen someone on the bridge. As for the lady in white I'd seen my first night at Sutherland Castle, I suppose he had every right to doubt it. After all, I doubted it, too, chalking it up to my imagination.

But had it been only that, my imagination? She'd spoken to me. Or was that imagination also, my ears playing tricks?

We reached the river and parked next to Constable McKay's car. He and Rufus Innes were far downstream, almost out of sight.

"I fell upstream," I said. "Near that bridge."

"That's where you saw the man?" George asked.

"What man?" Mort asked.

I repeated to him what had happened to me.

"Somebody tried to kill you, Mrs. F.?"

"I don't know what the motive was, but yes, someone did throw a log at me while I was in the water."

"This is a police matter," Mort said.

"That's why Constable McKay was called," George said.

"If this guy threw the log at you from this here bridge, why are they all the way down there?" Mort asked.

"Probably looking for my rod."

"Uh-huh," Mort said. "Let's take a look up on that bridge."

I glanced at George, whose face said nothing. But I knew what he was thinking. Mort obviously forgets that George is one of Scotland Yard's top inspectors. His restraint in reminding Cabot Cove's sheriff of that has always struck me as admirable.

The wooden bridge was wide enough for a vehicle to cross the river, but only barely. As we stepped onto it, its rickety structure was evident.

"Maybe we all shouldn't go on it at once," Seth Hazlitt suggested.

I was already on it, and continued to center span. George and Mort accompanied me; Dr. Symington, Ken Sassi, and Seth remained onshore.

"Where did you fall?" George asked.

I went to the shaky railing and pointed to the spot in the water where I'd been when the log was thrown.

"How close did it come to hitting you?" George asked.

"Close" was my response. "I had to twist my body to avoid it. That's why I fell."

"And you say it was quite large. Six feet long? A half a foot wide?"

"I think so. It happened so fast."

"Would take a person of considerable strength to throw such an object that distance," George said. He turned to Mort, who was examining the opposite railing. "Wouldn't you agree, Sheriff Metzger?"

"What?"

"It would take a strong person to throw a large log to where Jessica was fishing."

"*Ayuh*. I suppose it would. Look here, Mrs. F."

George and I went to where Mort stood at the opposite railing and leaned forward to see what he was pointing at. It was a cross carved into the wood. A pinkish brown stain defined the interior grooves of the symbol.

George touched his pinky to one of the cross's lines, withdrew it, and examined it. Nothing.

"Looks like dried blood," Mort said.

"Yes, I suspect it is," George said. "No telling how long it's been here, although it doesn't look terribly old to me."

"Looks like fresh cuts in the wood, though," Mort said.

"It does appear that way. I suggest we wait until Constable McKay examines it."

"Does Wick have a forensic lab?" I asked.

"No. But he can send it to Inverness, or Glasgow."

"Do you think it was carved by the person who threw the log at me?" I asked.

"A distinct possibility."

We felt the bridge move as Dr. Symington joined us. He looked at the carved cross and shook his head. "I was afraid of this," he said solemnly.

"Why do you say that, Doc?" Mort asked.

"Its symbolism," he said, running his index finger over the cross.

"I wouldn't touch that, Doc," Mort said. "It's evidence."

"Yes," Symington said. "Evidence of what is really going on here."

"Which is?" George asked. "What, in your opinion, Doctor, is really going on here?"

Symington looked up at George and gave him a tight smile. "Witchcraft, of course."

"What's the cross got to do with witchcraft?" Mort asked.

"It's been carved here to ward off a spell."

Seth now started across the bridge in our direction, causing it to creak and moan and sway.

"Let's get off before we all end up in the water," Mort said.

As we stood on the riverbank, Constable McKay and Rufus Innes approached. My heart tripped when I saw Rufus carrying my fishing rod. "You found it," I said, my voice mirroring my pleasure.

"Yes, ma'am," Rufus said, handing it to me. "Got itself wedged between some rocks. Doesn't look the worse for wear."

"Thank you," I said. "It means a lot to me."

"Been on the bridge, Horace?" George asked the constable.

"Not yet."

"Let me show you something."

Mort quickly said, "I found it, Constable. I'll show it to you."

George sighed and leaned against a tree as Mort led McKay to the middle of the bridge. They returned a minute later.

"Think you want to cut it out and send it off for analysis?" George asked.

"Nothing to be gained by that," McKay said. "Won't tell us anything we don't already know."

"It will confirm whether it's blood," George said. "And how long it's been there."

McKay's face said he didn't enjoy being told what to do when it came to police work.

"Mrs. Fletcher almost died here today because someone threw a log at her from that bridge," George said. "Whoever did that might have carved that cross as a signature of sorts. Dr. Symington says it could be an attempt to ward off a curse, or some other such thing. Not that I believe in such nonsense, but—"

"All right," McKay said. "I'll send Bob up here in the morning with a saw, cut it out a' the railing, send it to Inverness. Anything else you want me to do?" His words were fat with sarcasm.

"Not at the moment," George said. To Rufus Innes: "Much obliged, Rufus, for finding Mrs. Fletcher's rod."

"Just sorry a good day of fishing turned out like it did," the gillie said. "Happy to take you out another day."

"How about tomorrow?" Ken Sassi asked.

Innes looked at me for a reaction.

"I'm afraid Mrs. Fletcher is committed all day tomorrow," George said.

I smiled. "Yes, that's right. Perhaps another day before we go home."

"Give me a call. Been slow lately. I have some days available."

We arrived back at the castle in time for the cocktail hour in the drawing room. Naturally, everyone asked about my mishap on the stream that day. I tried to pass it off as just a silly slip, but they'd all been told about the log, and wanted to know whether I thought the person who threw it had deliberately tried to hit me with it.

"I really don't know," I replied. "I prefer to think not."

I didn't want to talk about it, and sought the solace of a far corner where I could sip my white wine in peace. But Dr. Symington came up to me. "I hope I didn't upset you, Mrs. Fletcher, pointing out that the cross was probably carved there to ward off a witch's curse."

"No, you didn't, Dr. Symington. But I'd be interested in hearing more about your theory."

"Happy to, Mrs. Fletcher. You see, there are three basic classifications of witches. White, gray, and black. The white witch is helpful to mankind, always wanting to provide some positive force. The gray witch is what one might term self-centered. Gray witches indulge themselves in magic and ritual, but have little interest one way or the other in helping or hurting men and women not possessed. But then there is the black witch."

His eyes opened wide as he sipped his drink and smiled knowingly.

"Ah, yes, the black witch. Black witches make their covenant with the Devil himself. Satan. They agree to inject evil into everything they can, to hurt and destroy all that is good. They sign what might be considered a legal agreement with Satan—sign it in their own blood—and surrender their body and souls to him. This occurs when Satan comes to earth as an ordinary man dressed in black. The witch signs her agreement with him, and he gives her a coin to seal the deal, as it were. The witch is also given a living symbol of her newfound power, usually a black cat, whose function is to aid her in spreading evil on earth. The cat's basic nourishment is to draw and drink blood from its mistress."

I forced a laugh to cover my increasing nervousness. "An interesting fable," I said.

"Fable? Hardly, Mrs. Fletcher. Witchcraft is not a fable. No, far from it. It is as real as you and I standing here talking. Do you know what I think?"

"I'm almost afraid to ask."

"I think the cross was carved, and outlined in blood, by someone who thought *you* were a witch whose powers had to be curtailed."

I looked for George, who wasn't there at the

time. The others were engaged in happy conversation in other parts of the large room.

"Dr. Symington, you don't really believe that, do you?"

"I do not disbelieve it, Mrs. Fletcher."

"Well, I can assure you that I have never cut a deal with the Devil, nor do I own a black cat."

"Never?"

"Well—years ago. A stray black cat I rescued and kept. But if you think that means—"

"Mrs. Fletcher, as with vampires, the Christian cross, especially when traced with blood, has always been considered an effective way of warding off a witch's curse."

"Excuse me, Doctor. I have to tell—something to—someone—over there."

I went to where Pete Walters and Seth Hazlitt were engaged in a spirited political debate. "Mind if I join you?" I asked.

" 'Course not, Jessica," Seth said. "Feelin' okay? You look white as a ghost."

"A witch, according to Dr. Symington. But a good witch."

"What are you talking about?" Pete said.

"A lecture on witches I just received from Dr. Symington."

Pete Walters leaned close to me and said, "The guy's nutty as a fruitcake. So's his wife. A pair of whackos."

"Speakin' of folks tetched in the head, where's that Peterman couple?" Seth asked. "Haven't seen them around."

"Oh, Inspector Sutherland told me just a little while ago that they've gone to Glasgow. On business, he said."

"Don't miss 'em in the least," said Seth. "Disagreeable chap. Feel a little sorry for his wife. Hate to be married to someone like that."

"Don't worry about it, Seth," Pete said. "Unlikely you ever will be."

They slipped back into their debate—it turned out to be a running argument they'd been having for years over whether Cabot Cove should establish a commission to bring industry to the town; our new mayor, Jim Shevlin, was all for it, as was Pete Walters. Seth didn't like change of any sort—and I left the room in search of George.

I found him in his office, feet up on his desk, attention focused on the window and what lay beyond it.

"Mind if I interrupt your reverie?" I asked.

"Not at all, Jessica." He removed his feet from the desk and leaned his elbows on it.

"Something wrong?" I asked.

He laughed as though he'd just been asked the most ludicrous question in the world: "Wouldn't you say something was wrong?"

"Because I fell in the stream?"

"Because someone *caused* you to fall. I just got off the phone with a man in London who's been trying to buy Sutherland Castle for the past few years."

"You told me there were interested buyers."

"And he's one of the most interested. Heads a business consortium with millions of pounds to spend. I think much of it comes from foreign investors. Arabs. The Japanese."

"Why are you telling me this, George?"

"Because I think I'll take him up on his offer."

"That's quite a serious decision to make. Sure you aren't overreacting to what happened today?"

"I don't think so. I don't want to make such a decision based upon emotion. And I'm sure you can understand why I'm not keen on having foreigners buy the castle. I'd like to see it, and Wick, remain in Scottish hands. But—"

"May I make a suggestion?"

"You know you can always do that."

"Sleep on it. Give it a few days. Don't act impetuously."

"A good thought, Jessica, but—"

"For *me*, George. I would hate to see you give up something so dear to you because of a series of silly mishaps to me and my friends. Wait until we're gone. You'll be able to think more clearly then."

"Sage advice, as might be expected from you."

"If it's sage advice, take it. I think dinner is ready. You are joining us?"

"Yes. Of course. Don't mind me, Jess. Just a momentary lapse in confidence. Come. Mrs. Gower has cooked up haggis for us. She makes the best in Wick."

Haggis? I thought as we went to announce to the others that dinner was about to be served. That traditional Scottish concoction whose ingredients, coupled with how it's prepared, strikes fear in the hearts of almost everyone visiting Scotland.

I stopped him just before we entered the drawing room. "George," I said, "I'm sure Mrs. Gower makes the best haggis in the world. But I'm afraid my friends from Maine might not—no, let me be honest—I'm afraid *I* might not like it."

It was the biggest laugh of the day from him, and I loved hearing it. "Jessica," he said, "I learned years ago that haggis is not to the liking of most visitors. Mrs. Gower serves it up once a week for those adventurous enough to want to taste our national culinary treasure. But I always insist that she have ready plenty of plain roasted chicken. Just in case."

Chapter Sixteen

Robert Burns, the revered Scottish poet, once called haggis "great chieftain o' the pudding race."

I'm not sure I would wax as poetic about Scotland's national dish as Mr. Burns. It's an off-putting culinary concoction (unless you were brought up with it as Mr. Burns was), falling into the pudding category but like no other pudding I've ever experienced.

Our gourmet chef, Charlene Sassi, told us at dinner that there were many different variations on the basic theme. But, in general, haggis consists of the liver, heart, and tongue of a sheep, combined with suet, onions, and lots of oatmeal, wrapped in the sheep's paunch, its stomach lining. It's boiled for about three hours and served whole on the plate, usually accompanied by mashed potatoes and vegetables.

Mrs. Gower personally, and with pride, served

her version of haggis, plopping down each plate before us with conviction. After the last of us had been served, she departed the dining room, leaving us to look at our meal, and at each other.

"It's really very good," Charlene said. "Don't let appearances deceive you."

"It's not the appearance," Seth Hazlitt said. "It's knowin' *what* I'm lookin' at that matters."

George sat at the head of the long table, a bemused smile on his lips.

"Do you like haggis, Inspector?" Susan Shevlin asked.

"*Ay*. I don't make a habit of it, but I enjoy a hearty haggis on occasion."

"Well, I'm not going to let it get cold," Charlene said. With that, she cut into the paunch, allowing the juices to burst forth onto her plate. She raised her fork, said, "*Bon appétit*," and put the food in her mouth.

We watched her the way people fixate on a sword swallower, or fire-eater. She chewed, swallowed, smiled, and said, "Excellent. My compliments to the chef."

Jim Shevlin said, "I think I'll try it. Hate to be accused of not being adventurous when it comes to food." He took his first bite and closed his eyes while swallowing.

"How is it?" his wife, Susan, asked.

"Different. Obviously an acquired taste."

"Jess?" Roberta Walters said. "Are you going to try it?"

Mort Metzger saved me from having to answer. "Anything else on the menu tonight?" he asked George Sutherland.

"Roast chicken."

"Sounds good to me," Seth said. "Maybe heat this haggis up and have it another day."

"Mrs. Gower will be disappointed," said Charlene as she continued to dig in.

"She'll understand," George said. "You're not the first group to request chicken." He went to the kitchen to tell Mrs. Gower to heat up chicken for all except himself, Charlene Sassi, and Jim Shevlin.

We enjoyed salad until the chicken was served by an especially dour Mrs. Gower, who said nothing in response to our feeble attempts to explain away our decision.

Unlike previous evenings, we didn't retire en masse to the drawing room for after-dinner cocktails. Everyone seemed to have other things to do, including me. I decided to use the evening to finish reading Malcolm James's manuscript, *Who Killed Evelyn Gowdie?*, and to try to sort out the events of that day on the river. That I'd almost drowned had been pushed to the back of my mind by the ensuing activities. But now, as I excused myself and went to my room, its impact seeped back into my consciousness. It wasn't an especially welcome feeling.

George Sutherland asked whether I wanted anything brought to my room. Tea sounded appealing; he said he'd have Fiona bring it to me after she'd finished helping Mrs. Gower clean the kitchen.

I opened one of the windows and looked down onto the front courtyard. The weather had changed again, no surprise, based upon northern Scotland's reputation. It felt as though a blanket of warm, humid air had settled in over Wick and the castle, a summerlike evening back home. I didn't especially like it. I was getting used to brisk, wet weather, and preferred that it stay that way for the duration of our visit to Sutherland Castle.

Any apprehension I experienced was mitigated by the pleasant contemplation of spending the next day alone with George. It seemed that the only periods of calm were when he was around, his large presence and low-key manner a welcome contrast to the series of upsetting incidents occurring since our arrival.

It was good to have electricity again. I pulled up a small stuffed chair next to a floor lamp by the open window, opened Malcolm James's manuscript on my lap, and started reading Chapter Two. While the first chapter had been a straightforward exposition of the bare facts of Evelyn Gowdie's death by pitchfork twenty years ago, the book now shifted into a fiction mode, in which Malcolm's detective character comes on the scene and begins investigating the murder.

I found myself engrossed as I read. Malcolm showed considerable promise as a novelist. He drew his characters with care into three-dimensional people. He set scenes nicely, giving just enough detail to place the reader in the action without abusing his descriptive powers.

Because I quickly became lost in my reading, I didn't hear the knock on my door at first. I did the second time, and went to it. Fiona stood in the hallway holding a tray with a teapot, cup and saucer, and a small plate of fudge.

"Come in," I said. "The fudge looks yummy."

"The what?" she asked as she brought the tray to the table next to my chair.

"The fudge." I pointed to it.

"Oh," she said with a gay laugh. "The *tablet*."

"That's what you call it?"

"*Ay*. And fudge, too. Homemade. Mrs. Gower herself."

"I suppose I'll have to succumb to my sweet tooth. Help yourself, Fiona. I'll only be having a piece or two."

"Thank you, Mrs. Fletcher. My sweet tooth is a very large one."

"And you have the slim figure to indulge it."

She curtsied, holding the hem of her pretty knee-length yellow-and-white-flowered dress out to the sides, which made me smile. I liked this girl.

"This is my favorite room in the whole castle," she said. "I like coming here to make the bed and such."

"You sound like you enjoy working at Sutherland Castle."

"Oh, I do. Some chores I dislike, but you can't always choose which ones you'll do, not when you're being paid to do them. Mrs. Gower keeps us running, that she does."

"Do you report to her?"

"*Ay*. And to Forbes sometimes."

"And to Malcolm?" I asked, eyebrows raised, levity in my voice.

Her giggle was infectious. "He told me he talked to you about us."

"That's right," I said. "He seems like a very nice young man. And a good writer, I might add. I'm reading his novel."

"You like it? You really do?"

"So far."

"We're so excited. He has a publisher."

"He does?"

"Yes. We just heard about it last night."

"That's wonderful," I said. "Would you like to sit down, Fiona?"

"Oh, I think I'd better get downstairs. Mrs. Gower will be looking for me."

"You work day and night?"

"Some days. Depends. I have to work tonight because Forbes took the rest of the evening off."

"He seems like a—how shall I say it?—he seems—"

"Crazy? Dilapidated?"

"Dilapidated?"

"Crazy."

"Oh. I hadn't heard that term used quite that way before." I thought back to Mort Metzger's comment before we left home about Americans and British speaking the same language, yet not always seeming to.

"I don't want to keep you from your work, Fiona, but Malcolm told me about the problems he's having with your mother because of all the talk of curses and witches in Wick, and at this castle."

She laughed. "Mum is superstitious, Mrs. Fletcher. Believes in all this nonsense that's been going on for years. Malcolm, too. He believes it, I think."

"He says his father does."

"*Ay*. Seems like everyone does. Except me."

I nodded. "I don't believe it. That makes two of us. But Malcolm says he's actually afraid for you working here at Sutherland Castle."

"No need for him to be. Because Daisy Wemyss was murdered? Some sick person killed her, that's for sure. Probably not even from Wick. Somebody passing through. That's the way I see it."

"I hope you're right. Fiona, have you seen the so-called lady in white here at the castle?"

"Her? Never have, not likely I will." Another giggle. "Too much a' the *baurley bree*, I think."

"Does that mean whiskey?"

"*Ay*. It does. I'll have you speakin' in the Scottish tongue yet."

"I look forward to it."

"May I ask you a question, Mrs. Fletcher?"

"Of course."

"Providing you don't think me too forward."

"I'll try not to."

"Are you and the inspector—?" She covered her mouth with her hands and looked at the floor, then back up at me. "Are you and Inspector Sutherland having a bit of a *screed*?"

"I'm not fluent in Gaelic yet, Fiona. Translate."

"Mrs. Gower says you and the inspector are havin' yourselves a romantic fling."

"Does she, now?"

"Everybody's talking about it."

"Are they?"

"I have to admit I can see it in your eyes. In his eyes, too. Hard to miss."

"Well, Fiona, I hate to dispel any juicy gossip,

but Inspector Sutherland and I are simply good friends. That's it. Sorry to disappoint.''

''All right.'' Her expression said she was placating me, not believing a word of my denial of any romantic relationship with George.

''Well, Fiona, thank you for the tea and the plate of—*tablet*?''

''You've got it, Mrs. Fletcher. I'd best be going before the old shrew gets to yelling for me.'' She grabbed two pieces of fudge from the plate, went to the door, and opened it. ''Good night, Mrs. Fletcher. Glad you like Malcolm's writing. He'll be famous one day, and I'll be his proud wife.''

I didn't try to fight my sweet tooth. I savored a piece of fudge with my tea and returned to reading Malcolm James's novel. Time passed quickly. I finished it, took off my glasses, and leaned back in the chair to contemplate what I'd read.

Malcolm really hadn't ended the story because, I suppose, there wasn't a closure to Evelyn Gowdie's murder twenty years ago. Malcolm's fictitious detective character worked the case up to the point where he'd identified a number of suspects in the community. Malcolm had inserted a final handwritten page on which he'd made notes to himself concerning integrating Daisy Wemyss's murder into the overall story. I was disappointed he hadn't wrapped things up. After all, he was writing fiction. Ending his story didn't depend upon a real solution to the actual murder. I couldn't help wonder why a publisher would commit to a first novel without the ending having been written. Probably because the rest of the manuscript showed such promise. The story woven by Malcolm James was compelling, taut, a proverbial page-turner.

I mentally reviewed the suspects he'd developed. One in particular stayed with me: a woman who aroused the detective's suspicions because she was one of only a few people who knew where Evelyn Gowdie would be when she was killed.

Thinking of her caused me to turn my attention to Rufus Innes, the gillie who'd guided Ken and me that day. As far as I could tell, he was the only person who knew we'd be going to that particular river, and that we would be fishing near the bridge from which the log was thrown. At least I assumed he was the only one who knew where we'd be.

Maybe he'd told others where he intended to guide us.

Maybe he was known to always take fishing clients' there. No, he'd made a point of telling us that he and his fellow guides seldom took clients there. But he took us there that day. He even directed me to the spot in the river near the bridge where someone was waiting.

But *was* someone waiting there for me? Perhaps not. Whoever threw that log might have come along *after* I was in the water and fishing near the bridge. And I had to accept the possibility that the log wasn't aimed at me. Maybe it was a kid throwing it into the water just for the fun of it, not realizing anyone was down there.

Conjuring such scenarios proved to be fatiguing, so I decided to go downstairs to see if any of my Cabot Cove contingent was still up. I found Seth Hazlitt sitting in front of the fireplace reading a book he'd found in one of the castle's many bookcases.

"Still awake, Jessica?"

"Yes. I was reading. I see you are, too. Good book?"

"*Ayuh*. About Robert Burns. Died at thirty-seven, poor fella. Lived near a seaside town called Ayr for most of his short life. Loved it there evidently. Wrote this about the town. '*Auld Ayr, wham ne'er a town surpasses, For honest men and bonny lasses.*' Bonny lasses. I like that."

"It does have a nice ring to it."

"Gotten over your episode on the river?"

"I think so."

"Still don't have any idea who might 'a thrown that log at you?"

"I'm not even sure someone did. I mean, someone did—throw the log—but maybe it wasn't intended to hit me."

Seth raised his eyebrows the way he always does when doubting me.

"I just don't know," I said defensively. "It all happened so fast. Maybe Constable McKay will know more after they cut the cross out of the bridge's railing."

He stared into the fire, brow knitted, lips pursed.

"How much for your thoughts?" I asked. "You've never given them away for a penny."

He slowly turned and looked at me, locked his eyes on mine. "Jessica, we've been friends for a very long time."

"We certainly have."

"And I've lived through most of your misadventures, either because I was with you, or heard about it over the television or radio."

I squeezed his arm. "And you've been staunch and loyal at every turn, Dr. Seth Hazlitt, for which this particular lady has always been very grateful. Now, what's your point?"

"My point is, Jessica, I'm not at all comfortable staying here."

I sighed. "I suppose I can't say I don't understand. But despite the things that have happened since we arrived, I'm actually having a good time."

"Of course you are, considerin' you get to spend time with George Sutherland."

I cocked my head and didn't attempt to keep a smile from forming. "And what does that mean?" I asked.

"Oh, I don't know Jessica. It just seems to me that you and the handsome Scotland Yard Inspector have an obvious mutual respect for each other."

"Why shouldn't we?"

He held up his hand. "Of course you should. Anything beyond respect, Jessica?"

"Romance, you mean?"

"*Ayuh*. Always known you had pretty strong feelings for him. Knew that years ago when you met him in London. Fairly obvious to any astute friend. I know you pretty well."

"You certainly do. But do you know what, Seth?"

"What?"

"As much as I adore you—and you know I do—I really don't think whatever feelings I might have for George to be—of interest to anyone but me."

"And him, of course."

"Yes. And George. Of course."

"Just don't want to see you get your feathers singed, Jessica. Only reason I bring it up."

"I don't have any feathers, Seth."

" 'Course you do. Every beautiful woman's got

'em. You're no exception. I'm sure Sutherland has noticed 'em.''

"I think it's bedtime," I said, standing.

"A little sleepy myself." He stood and clamped a hand on each of my arms. "Just want you to know that I'm always here for you, no matter what happens. You remember that, *heah*?"

"Yes, Seth. I *heah* loud and clear. Good night."

I made sure I was out of his sight before I dabbed at a tear that had formed in my left eye, and was running down my cheek. He was such a dear friend, and had been for many years.

And he was jealous of George.

Chapter Seventeen

At first, I wasn't awake enough to discern what I was touching. It was warm and soft.

I removed my hand and turned over, felt a cramp in my leg and returned to my original position. I opened one eye. Sunlight was streaming through the open window. Good, I thought in my sleepy haze. A pretty day to spend with George. I smiled, and stretched.

My hand touched it again. I closed my fingers. It moved. It made a sound. And then I felt the prick of pain on the back of my hand.

I sat bolt-upright and looked to where my hand had been, then at my hand itself. A slender trickle of blood ran from a tiny cut up near the wrist down over my knuckles.

I didn't want to scream, but it was involuntary, erupting from my throat.

My vocal reaction sent the big fat black cat flying to the floor and to the window.

"Get out!" I shouted.

The cat turned, arched its back, hissed at me, and disappeared onto a narrow ledge that ran the length of the exterior castle wall.

I sat in bed and tried to recover my composure, telling myself over and over that it was just a cat that had undoubtedly entered the room through the window I'd left open, and who'd decided to share my warm bed. I grabbed a tissue from the nightstand and pressed it against the scratch.

A black cat.

"The witch is also given a living symbol of her new-found power, usually a black cat, whose function is to aid her in spreading evil on earth. The cat's basic nourishment is to draw and drink blood from its mistress."

Dr. Symington had said that to me the previous evening.

"What happened to you, Mrs. F.?" Mort Metzger asked as I entered the dining room holding a tissue against my hand.

"I had company last night," I replied. "Anyone have a Band-Aid?"

"I do," Maureen Metzger said, pulling one from her purse and handing it to me.

"Best put some antibacterial cream on it," Seth Hazlitt said. "Got some in my room. Back in a second."

"What visitor?" Jim Shevlin asked.

"A big fat black cat. I left the window open when I went to bed, and he must have come through it."

Dr. and Mrs. Symington sat at the far end of the table. "A *black* cat?" he asked in his reedy voice.

"Yes."

He stared at me with beady eyes, causing me to avert my gaze. What did he think the experience represented, that I was a witch, and the black cat confirmed it by drawing blood? What nonsense.

"You okay, Jess?" Charlene Sassi asked.

"What? Oh, yes. Why?"

"You looked like you did at dinner the other night. You know, zoned out."

"Someplace else," Ken Sassi said. "Please pass the sausages."

"Pancakes or eggs, Mrs. Fletcher?" Forbes asked somberly. I hadn't realized he was behind me.

His voice startled me. "Oh. Ah, neither, please. Just fruit, and some cereal if you don't mind."

"Where's our host?" Pete Walters asked.

"Inspector Sutherland went to town," Forbes answered before disappearing through the door to the kitchen.

"Tell us more about the cat," Roberta Walters said. "Why did he scratch you?"

Seth returned with a tube of cream, and carefully squeezed out a small amount onto the scratch. "That been washed good?" he asked. I confirmed that it had been. He applied the Band-Aid over the cream, admiring his handiwork.

"Did it bite you, or scratch you?" Jed Richardson asked.

"Scratched me, I think."

Forbes brought me my breakfast. "Do you know when Inspector Sutherland plans to return?" I asked him.

"No, ma'am."

"Do you know why he went into town?"

"No, ma'am." To the group: "Would anyone care for anything else?"

A negative response from everyone at the table.

"What's on tap for everyone today?" I asked as we went from the dining room to the large parlor, where a fire glowed in the fireplace. It was chilly in the castle, but Jed and Alicia had taken an early morning walk and reported it was shaping up to be a warm and humid day.

No one seemed to have any specific plans, except me. "George and I planned to spend the day together," I said when asked how I intended to spend my day. "He has a favorite pub he wants me to see. Other sights in the area, too, I imagine. I just wonder why he—"

"Probably had some business to tend to," Seth said, anticipating what I was thinking. "Probably be back momentarily."

"I suppose so," I said.

"Mrs. Fletcher."

I turned to face Dr. Symington. "Yes?"

"A word alone with you, please?"

"Oh, Doctor, I think I forgot to do something in my room. Perhaps another time. At dinner? Over cocktails?"

"I don't think it can wait," he said.

"Well, I think—"

Malcolm James entered the room. "Excuse me," he said, "but has anyone seen Fiona this morning?"

We looked at each other and shrugged.

"I just thought—"

"Is she missing?" I asked. "Was she supposed to be here at work this morning? She worked late last night. Maybe she—"

"Her mum called. She never returned home last night."

"Mrs. Fletcher, perhaps if we could—"

I cut Dr. Symington off by saying to Malcolm, "There must be a reasonable explanation for it. Maybe she stayed overnight with a friend."

"She wouldn't do that without telling her mum first," he said.

I was sure he was right. The only thing I could think of at the moment was Daisy Wemyss, Fiona's predecessor on the castle's staff, whose body I'd found in Wick.

"Excuse me," Malcolm said, fairly running from the room.

I followed him to the kitchen, where Mrs. Gower was stirring something in a large metal pot on the stove.

"The guests haven't seen her," Malcolm told her.

"Like all the rest," Mrs. Gower said, continuing to stir. "Can't depend on any *younker* these days to show up for work."

I assumed she meant youngster.

"Did anyone see her leave last night?" I asked.

"No," Malcolm answered. "Forbes left early. And Mrs. Gower—"

The stout and stern lady stopped stirring, turned, and said, "You mind your own business, young man. Don't be tellin' anybody what I did or where I was."

I motioned with my finger for Malcolm to follow me out of the kitchen. Once away from Sutherland Castle's formidable cook, I asked him, "Do you know why Inspector Sutherland went into town this morning?"

"No. I saw him leave. He didn't say anything."

"All right. Now, back to Fiona. Can you think of anywhere in town, anyone in town who might have seen her last night?"

"She has friends."

"And you know who they are?"

"*Ay.* Some of 'em."

"And have you checked the castle thoroughly?"

"That's not an easy thing to do, Mrs. Fletcher. It's a real *beezer.*"

"Beezer?"

"It's a big place, Mrs. Fletcher. Very big."

He was right, of course. What concerned me most was that if Fiona was in some dark recess of Sutherland Castle, it couldn't be for any good reason. I wrapped my arms about myself as a sudden chill stabbed me deep inside.

"Well, Malcolm, it may be big, but I'm going to start looking. I'll get my friends to help. I suggest you go into town and contact Fiona's friends."

"*Ay.* I'll do that straight away."

The swinging kitchen doors swung open, and Mrs. Gower emerged. "Where's the wood I told you to get?" she asked Malcolm.

"I was busy looking for Fiona, Mrs. Gower, and—"

"Look in the nearest pub is my suggestion. You forget about her and get to your chores."

"Mrs. Gower," I said, "I really think that Malcolm—all of us for that matter—should—"

"You may be a guest, Mrs. Fletcher," she said. "You may be some high-and-mighty writer. You may be the apple a' Mr. Sutherland's eye. But I'll thank you to leave the runnin' a' this house to me." She stepped back into the kitchen, the doors closing behind her.

"Whew!" I said.

"Don't pay her no mind, Mrs. Fletcher. She's just a natural old grump. I'll go to town while you look here for Fiona."

I returned to the living room, where Ken and Charlene Sassi and Jim and Susan Shevlin were still congregated. I told them about Fiona, and suggested we split up to search for her at the castle. "Why don't you check the grounds, Ken," I said. "Jim and Susan can go upstairs. Charlene and I will take this floor."

As Charlene and I moved out, we ran into Mort and Maureen Metzger.

"Where you going, Mrs. F.?" Mort asked.

I explained.

"I knew it," Mort said.

"Knew what?" Charlene asked.

"Knew there'd be more trouble."

"The important thing is to find Fiona," I said. "Ken is looking outside. Why don't you go help him?"

A half hour later, Charlene and I had come up empty. There was no sign of Fiona on the main floor. We'd checked every room and closet, beneath stairwells, every nook and cranny. Actually, I was relieved at our failure. I wasn't anxious to be the one to stumble upon her body as I had with Daisy Wemyss.

I suggested we go outside to see how Mort, Maureen, and Ken were faring. As we stepped through the front door to the central courtyard, Mort's voice came from afar. "Hey!" he shouted. "Over here!"

He was behind a stable, one of a number of outbuildings on the grounds. We rounded the rear corner of the building just as Ken and Maureen came from the other side. Mort was bent over something beneath a shed roof attached to the stable's back wall.

I grabbed Charlene's arm to stop her from getting any closer. I was certain Mort had found Fiona's body, and didn't want to subject Charlene to the shock of it. No, not entirely truthful. I didn't want to subject *myself* to it.

Mort saw us holding back and said, "Come over here, Mrs. F. and tell me what you make of this."

"Is she—?"

"Is she what?"

"Nothing," I said, walking toward him.

He was looking at a dress we all remembered Fiona having worn the night before, a pretty white-and-yellow-flowered print. A vision of her curtsying in my room came and went.

"Look over there," Ken Sassi said, pointing to

a pair of shoes. No question about it. They were the shoes Fiona wore when she visited my room.

Before I could admonish them not to touch anything, Ken picked up one of the shoes. His fingers came away with a sticky substance on them. He showed them to us. Blood.

"But no sign of her," Mort said.

"What do we do?" Charlene asked.

"Get back to the house and report this to Constable McKay," I said. "Maybe I can find out where George went."

"Should we take these things back with us?" Ken asked.

"No," I said. "We've disturbed the scene enough. Let the police take care of it."

"Absolutely right," Mort said. "This here is a crime scene. I'll rustle up some rope and cordon it off."

"Good idea," Ken Sassi said to our sheriff.

We returned to the castle, where I asked Forbes, who was dusting furniture in the living room, for McKay's telephone number. He made it obvious he didn't appreciate being interrupted, but left the room, returning a minute later with the number on a piece of paper. I took it from him and went to George's office to call the constable.

"McKay here."

"This is Jessica Fletcher. I was the one who—"

"I have a decent memory, Mrs. Fletcher."

His snide comment took me aback. But I forged ahead. "Are you aware that Fiona, the young woman who works here at Sutherland Castle, is missing?"

"*Ay.* I've heard."

"Well, we've just found her dress, and a bloody pair of her shoes, behind a stable on the castle's grounds."

"Have you, now?"

I kept my anger in check. "Yes, we have," I said icily.

"Well, as soon as Bob gets back from cutting the cross out a' the bridge railing, I'll send him up to take a look."

"That's very kind of you. Do you know where Inspector Sutherland is?"

"*Ay.*"

I waited for him to elaborate. It didn't come. "Where is he?" I asked.

"Should be back to the castle by now. Left here a half hour ago."

"He was with you?"

"*Ay.*"

"Thank you."

The minute I hung up, George came through the door.

"I was just trying to track you down," I said.

"I was in town."

"I know. I just got off the phone with Constable McKay."

"I was with him."

"So he said. You know about Fiona?"

"I certainly do. No one has seen her?"

"George, we found her dress and her shoes behind the stable. There was blood on her shoes."

He winced. "Good Lord," he said. "Another."

"But we haven't found *her*. That means there's hope."

He slumped in a chair across the desk from me, formed a tent with his hands, and lowered his chin to it. He was gray; fatigue and worry were etched on his handsome face.

"I'm selling Sutherland Castle," he said, his voice so low I could barely make out his words.

"I thought—"

"I know. You suggested I wait until you and your friends had left. But the representatives from the London real estate consortium arrived in Wick last night. They've upped their offer. I met with them for breakfast this morning."

"It's definite?"

"Well, almost. I had reservations, and told them I needed another twenty-four hours to think it over. But then I bumped into McKay, who told me Fiona was missing. And now, you tell me you found her clothing, bloody at that. If anything has made up my mind, Jessica, it's this. The proverbial straw to break this camel's back. It's best I *put the peter on it.*"

"Which means?"

"Put a stop to the madness."

"It's your decision, George. But I can't help thinking that—"

"Another murder, Jessica. Enough is enough."

"We don't know that Fiona has been murdered."

"Do you doubt it?"

"All I'm saying is that you not do something you might live to regret until we find out for certain what's happened to her."

"I don't know, Jessica. I just don't know."

"Constable McKay said he'd send his assistant here to look at the clothing—after he's finished cutting the cross from the bridge. Why don't *we* take a look?"

Mort had strung a rope around the area in which Fiona's dress and shoes were discovered. He'd hung strips of white cloth to make sure it was noticed.

We ducked beneath the rope, and George knelt to more closely observe the clothing. "Found exactly this way?" he asked.

"Not quite. Ken picked up a shoe. That's when we realized there was blood on it."

George stood. "It doesn't look good, does it?" he said sadly.

"We just don't know. Finding her clothing, and

finding her body are two different things. In fact, I can't help but wonder why this clothing is here."

"Meaning what?"

"It all seems—well, it seems a deliberate attempt to suggest the worst, without *showing* the worst."

"Why would anyone do that?"

"Why does anyone do anything, George? Like kill Daisy Wemyss."

"What happened to your hand?" he asked, noticing the Band-Aid.

"Oh, nothing. A cat got into my room last night. When I touched him this morning, he scratched me."

"What cat?"

"A big fat black one."

"That'd be Walter. Lives in the barn with other cats. Forbes feeds them. Should have warned you about leaving the window open at night. Walter likes to visit guests who do."

"It was nothing. Just a little scratch."

We walked slowly back to the castle and into the living room, where Forbes was again polishing furniture.

"Where's Malcolm?" George asked.

"I sent him to town to talk to Fiona's friends," I said.

"Good idea. Forbes, would you please fetch us tea?"

We said nothing as we sat in front of the fire and waited for Forbes to return. I broke the silence with, "Tell me more about these real estate people from London."

"Not much to tell. Very rich, for sure. They've been buying up country properties, most of them here in Scotland. They buy them up, fix them up, and turn them into profitable resorts."

"I can see why they'd want Sutherland Castle," I said.

"I can, too. I don't especially like the chaps they sent to Wick, but my personal feelings about them don't matter. Constable McKay told me this morning he's afraid the citizen group that's been trying to force me to sell might decide to take matters into their own hands now that Fiona is the next victim. Try to take over the castle by force."

"That's absurd," I said. "Surely, Constable McKay won't allow that."

"Not much he can do about it. Just him and Bob. I told him about my breakfast meeting, and that I was going to sell the castle. He was much relieved. Said it was the only way to avoid bloodshed."

"I can't believe in this day and age that citizens would be talking about storming a man's castle. That's—it's medieval. Barbaric."

The words of my British publisher, Archie Semple, came back to me: *"Still planning to venture to the land of the barbarians?"*

"What are you thinking?" George asked.

"That I don't want to lose the day we've planned together. I'd like to get away from here for a few hours. Go to that pub you love and have a quiet lunch."

"And we'll do it."

Bob, Constable McKay's deputy, arrived, accompanied by Constable McKay. After examining Fiona's dress and shoes, and carefully collecting them in plastic bags, they settled in the living room with us.

"We'll find her body soon, I fear," McKay said.

"Why wasn't her body with her clothes?" I said.

McKay and Bob looked at me. "What are you gettin' at?" McKay asked.

"It just doesn't make any sense, that's all," I said. "It's as though someone wants us—wants *somebody* to believe Fiona has been murdered, like Daisy Wemyss was. But until her body *is* found, all we have is her clothing."

"It's enough for me," McKay said. He looked at his deputy. "Enough for you, Robert?"

"*Ay*. Absolutely. Plenty for me."

"You'll be checking the blood on the shoes, I take it," George said.

"What for?" McKay replied. "We don't have her blood to compare it against."

"But what if it's not human blood?" I said, the possibility suddenly occurring to me.

McKay and Bob again looked at me as though I might be senile. "And what do you think red blood on a young woman's shoes might come from, Mrs. Fletcher?" the constable said, a smirk on his face.

"I don't know. An animal, perhaps. The point is that Inspector Sutherland is right. The blood should be checked."

"I'll be the judge a' that," McKay said.

"I'm sure you will," I said, unable to disguise my disgust with his attitude.

Malcolm James arrived minutes after McKay and his deputy had left.

"Any luck?" I asked him.

"No, ma'am. It's like Fiona just disappeared from the earth. Have you learned anything?"

George and I looked at each other. George said, "I'm afraid we've found Fiona's dress and shoes out behind the stable."

"Oh, no," Malcolm said.

"I'm afraid it's true," I added. "And there was blood on her shoe."

"Good *Guid*! Poor Fiona."

"It doesn't mean any harm has come to her, Malcolm," I said.

"What else could it mean?" he said. "Excuse me. I'd best see if Mrs. Gower *gie a heize*."

"What did he say?" I asked when he was gone.

"Odd expression. Archaic Gaelic. Lend her a hand, I think. I have a few things to tend to before we set off for lunch. I want to gather all the paperwork on the castle, deeds and such, for the London buyers."

"I suppose you should. I'll freshen up in my room. Meet you down here in an hour?"

"*Ay*. That'll be enough time."

"George."

"Yes."

"Whatever you decide to do, just know I'm proud to stand with you."

"You'll never know how much that means to this stubborn Scotsman, Jessica."

"Then, stay stubborn, George. Don't be too quick to give in. Stubborn becomes you."

Chapter Eighteen

I didn't need an hour to get ready for lunch, but I did want some time alone to attempt to factor in that morning's discoveries with everything else that had gone on in Wick and at Sutherland Castle.

I sat in a chair and tried to sort it out, but my attention kept shifting to the bagpipes I'd placed in a corner of the room. I considered blowing into them as a way of venting all the negative thoughts out of my body, but it loomed as too daunting a task.

Outside, Forbes tended one of the flower gardens, bent over, each stroke of the hoe slowly and steadily digging into the black earth. As I watched him, I realized how the events of the past few days had clouded my knowledge of, and appreciation for this spectacularly beautiful place in which I'd found myself. Circumstances had led me to come in contact only with the more bizarre elements of Wick and the castle. We didn't have that many days left, and I made a silent pledge to spend those days meeting the good and decent people of Wick, and drinking in the countryside in sufficient gulps to create lifetime memories.

Thinking positively has always buoyed my spirits when they've been low. It's like how the act of writing forces my mind to organize its thoughts. External actions influencing mood and spirit. I believe in it because it works, just as many of my actor and actress friends believe in costumes and makeup generating an internal sense of character.

Feeling better, I ventured downstairs. A peek into George's office showed him immersed in paperwork. I didn't disturb him. Instead, I wandered out into the courtyard, where Seth Hazlitt was now talking—attempting to talk is more accurate—with Forbes, who continued to hoe the garden.

"Jessica," Seth said. "How's the hand?"

"I'd forgotten about it," I said. "Fine."

"Got to watch for infection."

"I will."

"The man knows how to wield a hoe," Seth said, nodding at Forbes.

"You should know," I said. "You keep a nice garden."

"Gettin' tougher, though, as I get older."

"So I've noticed."

Seth stepped close to Forbes. "Say, Forbes, what sort a' plants do best up here in Scotland?"

He stopped digging, straightened up, and said, "Hearty ones. Excuse me. I have chores inside to tend to."

We watched him walk away and disappear around the side of the castle.

"That fella defines brooder," Seth said. "Sour sort."

"The Scots prefer dour."

"Doesn't matter what they prefer. I call him a brooder. What are you doin' here, Jessica? Thought you were heading off for the day with our host."

"We're leaving soon. You haven't heard, have you?"

"Heard what?"

"About finding Fiona's dress and shoes."

"Can't say that I have. The young man said she hadn't come home, but you know young people. What about her dress and shoes?"

I filled him in.

"Doesn't sound too promising, does it?"

"No. But the fact it's only her clothing, and not *her*, causes me to say it's premature to expect the worst."

"Jessica's famous jelly glass always bein' half full."

"If you prefer to view it that way. I have to catch up with George. What are you up to today?"

"Thought I'd just wander around, stroll into town. If I see the young woman Fiona, I'll let everybody know."

I smiled. "I hope you do see her, Seth. Enjoy yourself. I understand we're having a special dinner tonight."

"So I heard. What I'm really looking forward to is those Highland Games day after tomorrow. Always wanted to see them."

"I almost forgot about that. Sounds like fun."

"*Ayuh*, that it does. See you at supper."

George emerged from the castle wearing a houndstooth check jacket with leather at the elbows, tan slacks with razor-sharp creases, white shirt, red tie, red V-neck sweater, and boots polished to a high gloss. A pair of binoculars hung from a strap around his neck.

"Ready?" he asked.

"Yes. Just give me a minute to grab a sweater."

I ran into the castle and was about to go up the stairs to my room when my eye went to a pile of mail on a small table. I'm not a person who looks at other people's mail, but the envelope on top of the pile caused me to step closer to read to whom it was addressed, and who'd sent it. The number ten envelope was addressed to Malcolm James, in-care-of Sutherland Castle, Wick, Scotland. The return address read: "Flemming Publishing, Ltd."

As I ascended the stairs, I wondered why Malcolm would be receiving mail here, at his place of employment. As far as I knew, he lived in town with his mother. Maybe he gave this publishing company the castle address in order to impress. Was this the publisher Fiona said had expressed interest in his novel? Probably so.

I didn't give it another thought as I took my sweater from the closet and returned to the courtyard, where George had rolled out a vintage Mercedes I hadn't seen before from a four-car garage. It obviously wasn't driven much. Its black finish glowed from a recent waxing, and the engine purred.

"Care to drive?" George asked.

I laughed. "You know I don't drive."

"*Ay*, and I still wonder why you don't."

"Just never got around to it."

"I could teach you."

"Oh, no. Even if I wanted to learn, it wouldn't be here, where everyone drives on the wrong side of the road."

"That's presumptuous of you, Jessica. I think it's you Americans who use the wrong side."

"An argument that will never be resolved."

The interior of the car was as luxurious as the exterior was polished. We left the castle grounds and headed directly for the coastline. The sky was active: brilliant blue sky and puffy white clouds whisked along on stiff winds, then the sudden appearance of towering black thunderclouds. Rain could be seen falling from them in the distance, black streaks reaching the ground.

George stopped on the edge of a sheer granite bluff, got out, and opened the door for me. We stood on the precipice and looked out over the North Sea. The wind felt gale force, although I suppose it wasn't. I do know it was cold, and I pulled my cable-knit sweater closer around me. George noticed I was shivering, and added his arm to the sweater's warmth. We stood silently, the wind carrying seawater to sting our faces, eyes narrowed against it, smiles on our lips at the majesty of the moment.

"Being born here must mean carrying this remarkable place with you always," I said.

"*Ay*. It does get in your bones and soul."

"So beautiful. It's awe-inspiring."

"I'm glad you can see the beauty in it, Jessica, through the ugliness of the other things that have happened."

"I can," I said. "This is the way I want to remember Wick. This is the way I *will* remember it. This moment, this spot."

"And so shall I. Jessica, I—"

"I'm cold," I said.

"Let's get in the car. We'll go for lunch."

I knew George wanted to resume a conversation about his feelings for me, but I found it too painful to continue. It might have been selfish, but I wanted to enjoy the rest of my stay in northern Scotland in a simple way, unencumbered by the turmoil of deep personal feelings.

The pub George took us to was on the docks, near where Seth and I had had our confrontation with Evan Lochbuie. It was called the Birks of Aberfeldy.

"What an unusual name," I said.

"From a Burns poem, 'The Birks of Aberfeldy.' The birches of Aberfeldy, a Scottish town."

Inside, the atmosphere was warm and inviting. The long bar was two deep, and most of the tables were occupied. But there was a recently vacated one by the front window, which we took.

A waitress came to the table. "Good day, Inspector Sutherland," she said. She was a pretty, middle-aged woman with long black hair worn loose down her back, and sported an abundance of makeup. She wore black jeans and a yellow sweater beneath a large apron bearing the pub's name.

"Good day, Joan. This is Mrs. Fletcher, a good friend and my guest for a week or so."

I extended my hand. As she took it, Joan said, "I know all about you, Mrs. Fletcher."

"Oh?" I assumed she referred to my books.

"Not much to do here in Wick," she said. "Everybody's talking about you."

"Talking about—?"

"You and Inspector Sutherland." Her smile was knowing, with a trace of wickedness added.

I looked down at the table. George sensed my discomfort and quickly said, "We'll be looking at menus, Joan, if you don't mind. And hearing about today's specials."

She returned moments later and handed us each a handwritten menu. "Two specials today," she said. "Tripe and onions, and toad-in-the-hole. We've got beef and Yorkshire pudding, though the beef's a bit on the tough side, if you know what I mean."

"We'll need a few minutes," George said. "In the meantime, a drink, Jessica?"

"I suppose I should at least taste a beer."

"Two ales, please."

We perused the menu until Joan brought our beers. George lifted his glass: "To finally finding a few peaceful hours together."

"That's worth drinking to," I said, touching the rim of my glass to his. I tasted the ale. It was slightly bitter, but not unpleasant. I put it down and asked, "So, George, what is toad-in-the-hole?"

His laugh was a low rumble. "Sausages in batter. Quite good, actually. I'd take Joan's advice about the beef."

"Mad cow disease?"

"No. Tough-cut-of-beef disease. Like jellied eels?"

"No."

"Nor do I. There's always the plowman—chunk of cheese, crusty brown bread, butter, a few pickled onions."

"Dover sole and spinach sounds just fine," I said.

"We'll make it two."

We talked about many things as we waited for our lunch to be served. George finished his ale and ordered another. I allowed mine to sit.

After we were served—the sole was superb, as was the simple salad accompanying it—the conversation at the bar grew louder. It was impossible to ignore it. A large, heavyset man in workman's clothing seemed to be holding court with other gentlemen surrounding him. It soon became evident that he intended us to hear his words.

"... Brought terrible things to this fine village. A curse, that's what Sutherland Castle is. We should burn it down, rid ourselves of it."

His friends loudly agreed, slapping him on the back.

"Maybe we'd better leave," I said to George.

"We haven't had dessert," he said, his eyes trained on the big man at the bar. "They make very good sweets here."

"I'm sure they do. But—"

George called for Joan, our waitress. "What sweets are you serving up today?"

"Trifle. Gooseberry fool. Flitting dumpling."

"Translation needed," I said, smiling but keeping my eye on the bar, where the conversation about Sutherland Castle was increasing in fervor and volume.

"A 'fool' is a light, creamy sweet," George said. "Gooseberries are in season. A flitting dumpling is a stout pudding. We can slice it and take it along when we 'flit' to another place."

"That's wonderful," I said. "I'll have the gooseberry fool."

"Trifle for me," said George.

Joan leaned close to us. "Sorry about the boys, Inspector. They've had a wee bit too much ale."

"Not a problem," George said. "Coffee, J sica?"

"Yes, please."

"Two coffees. And a check."

Dessert was excellent, although my enjoyment of it was tempered by the rising tension in the Birks of Aberfeldy. Joan handed George the check. He placed money on it, got up, came around, and held out my chair for me to stand. As he did, the big man pushed away from the bar and walked unsteadily toward us. His eyes were watery and bloodshot, his mouth twisted with drunken anger.

"Good afternoon, sir," George said as he helped me on with my coat.

"You've got nerve, Sutherland, comin' down here into the village."

"And why might that be?" George asked.

The big man seemed unsure how to answer. He ran his tongue over his lips and blinked.

"Good day, everyone," George said, touching my elbow and guiding me in the direction of the door. I was aware that conversation had ceased in the pub, and that all eyes were on us.

The big man stepped into our path.

"Can I be of help to you?" George asked, locking eyes.

"*Ay.* You can sell that bloody castle and get yourself out of Wick." Some of his friends moved closer to the confrontation.

"I'll do *what* I wish, and do it *when* I wish," George said. "In the meantime, you're blocking our way. The lady doesn't appreciate it."

Now the big man's watery eyes turned to me. " 'The lady,' is she? Your lady, you mean."

"Get out of the way," George said. To me: "Go on, Jessica. Wait for me outside."

"I'll leave with you," I said.

George took my hand and made a move for the door, but the big man continued to step in our way, causing George to bump up against him.

It happened so fast. In one motion, George

pushed me away, then shoved his fist into our antagonist's chest. The big man growled and raised his arm to strike. But George was too fast. This time, his fist made contact with the big man's nose, sending him stumbling back into the arms of his friends, blood trickling down over his lip.

I retreated farther into a corner, anticipating a larger fight to break out. George stood firm, eyes trained on his opponent, fists clenched. The big man wiped blood from his face and muttered, "You broke my nose."

"You asked for it," George said. "Are we finished here?"

This was the moment of truth. Would the big man charge, or would he back off?

"Lunch was excellent, Joan," George said to our waitress, who stood with the bartender at the end of the bar. I noticed the bartender held a stout wooden shaft, just in case it was needed.

It wasn't. The big man cursed under his breath, turned, and leaned on the bar, his friends following suit.

Once outside, George drew a deep breath and rubbed his right hand with his left.

"You're hurt," I said.

"Nothing serious. No broken bones, except for his nose. Bloody fool. I hate fights, will walk miles to avoid one. I feel *black affrontit*, Jessica. Quite ashamed, subjecting you to violence."

"You could have arrested him."

"*Ay*. Any member of the Yard has jurisdiction throughout the U.K. Even here in Wick, as far north as you can get in Scotland except for John o' Groat's. But it wasn't a police matter. Stupid bloke is drunk. He's *cocked the wee finger* too many times."

I smiled, as I usually did when George slipped into his Scottish idiomatic speech. "Don't be ashamed," I said. "You did what you had to do."

"Feel like a walk, Jessica?"

"Yes. It's a nice day for it."

We strolled the dock area, breathing in the bracing salt air and reveling in the sun's warmth on our faces. George suddenly stopped, raised his binoculars to his eyes, and trained them on something in the distance.

"What is it?" I asked.

"A reed bunting. Not many of them around these days."

I saw what held his interest, a bird resting on a piling.

"I wondered why you were carrying those binoculars," I said. "Didn't know you were a birdwatcher."

"Strictly amateur, but I do enjoy spotting them." As he handed the binoculars to me, the bird flew away.

I put them to my eyes anyway and slowly

scanned the open water, where boats of varying sizes moved slowly in and out of the large harbor. I focused on one boat, went past it, then returned. It was Evan Lochbuie, the madman who'd caused Seth to fall overboard.

"Mr. Lochbuie is out there in his boat," I said, handing the binoculars to George. He trained them on the area I indicated with my finger. "That's interesting," he said.

"What is?"

"The fellow with him. Look."

I did, and saw a man in a business suit I hadn't seen the first time, standing next to Lochbuie at the boat's console. "Who is he?" I asked.

"One of the buyers from London I had breakfast with this morning."

"Oh? Why would he be out on a boat with someone like Evan Lochbuie?"

"I haven't an answer, Jessica. Maybe you can come up with one."

"Maybe I can. Still feel like walking?"

"I feel like doing anything except returning to the castle."

"Then, let's walk. While we do, I'll tell you what I think might be going on. More important, what we might do about it. I think it's time to bring this to a head."

Chapter Nineteen

Despite the beauty of the day, Fiona's disappearance, and the discovery of her clothing, took the edge off the pleasure of being together. Conversation inevitably returned to that unpleasant subject, and so we headed back to the castle sooner than originally planned. Constable McKay and his deputy, Bob, were there waiting for George.

"Hello, Horace," George said.

"Hello, George. Spare us a minute?"

"Of course. I'll catch up with you later, Jessica."

George escorted McKay and Bob to his office, and I went to my room. Malcolm James was just leaving it; he'd brought me ice, fruit, and a bottle of water.

My first question was, "Any word on Fiona?"

"No, ma'am. Everyone's searching for her. Constable McKay's here."

"Yes, I know. He's downstairs with Inspector Sutherland. You must be worried to death."

"*Ay*, that I am, Mrs. Fletcher. Sick over it."

"Wouldn't you be better off helping look for her, instead of working?"

"I'd rather be busy. Helps keep my mind off it."

"I understand. By the way, I hear congratulations are in order."

"For what?"

"An inopportune time to bring it up, I suppose, but I think it's wonderful news that you've found a publisher for your novel."

"What?"

"A publisher for *Who Killed Evelyn Gowdie?* Fiona told me about it last night."

"She did?" His expression was a combination of shock and concern.

"It isn't true?"

He smiled. "Oh, Fiona tends to exaggerate a wee bit. There's a publisher who's expressed some interest, that's all."

"That's certainly a fine start. I finished reading your manuscript, Malcolm. It's quite—it's very good, although I must admit I was disappointed that it lacks an ending."

"Just want to see how things turn out in real life," he said, poised to leave.

"But it's fiction," I said. "There's really no need to—"

"Excuse me, Mrs. Fletcher. Mrs. Gower'll be looking for me, mad as a hen."

I picked up Mickey Spillane's novel, which I hadn't finished, and went downstairs to find a chair outside, where I could continue reading it. I'd noticed a small wrought-iron bench behind a thick growth of bushes at the rear of the castle, and decided it would provide me the solitude I sought.

But as I circumvented the castle and came close to the spot, I heard a man and a woman's voice coming from it. It sounded like Malcolm to me, but I couldn't be sure. I took a few steps closer, but my attention was diverted by the sound of a truck's throaty engine, and tires on gravel.

The source of it came through an open rear gate. It was a big truck, followed by a car. As they passed me in the direction of the front courtyard, I read on the truck's side SPERLING VIDEO RENTALS. The car came abreast, driven by the Hollywood film producer, Brock Peterman. Tammy sat next to him.

I decided Mickey's book could wait, and followed the vehicles to where Brock Peterman stood with three young men, who'd climbed down from the truck's cab.

"Hello," I said, waving.

"What 'a you say?" Peterman said. He turned to the others: "This is the famous mystery writer, Jessica Fletcher."

Their blank faces said they hadn't heard of me, and didn't care that they hadn't.

"I picked up this crew in Edinburgh," Peterman said.

"Are you planning to make a movie here?"

"A documentary. This place is stranger than fiction. How about an interview with you in an hour? Hey, it just came to me. How about you hosting the show? Like they do on British TV Yeah, that's it!"

"Sorry, Mr. Peterman, but I wouldn't want to do that. Does Inspector Sutherland know of your plans?"

He shrugged.

"I think you should get his permission before unloading your equipment."

"Yeah, yeah, I will." He leaned into the open car window. "Hey, Tam, come on. You can't sit there all day."

"I'm almost finished," she said, continuing to buff her nails.

I went inside, where George, Constable McKay, and Deputy Bob had just come from the office and stood together in the foyer.

"Excuse me," I said, starting past them.

"You might want to hear this, Jessica," George said.

"Hear what?"

"The big bloke in the pub today wants to press charges against me for assault."

"That's preposterous," I blurted. "He went to hit you first."

"That's what I told the constable. But our fat friend says otherwise."

"Well, I assure you I'll be a witness if it ever comes to that. I'll fly here to testify from wherever I am."

"Probably won't come to that, Mrs. Fletcher," McKay said. "Think over what I said, George. Think hard and fast about it."

"I will," George said, his expression grave.

After they left, I said to George, "I take it they didn't come here just to tell you that the drunk in the pub wants to press charges."

"You're right. The constable says he can no longer be responsible for the safety of anyone at Sutherland Castle. According to him, the townspeople are ready to take matters into their own hands."

"Do you believe him?"

"I don't know. If I buy what you said this afternoon, Jessica, I probably shouldn't believe him. But I'm not sure."

We heard the warning *beep beep beep* trucks make when backing up.

"What the devil is that?" George asked.

"Mr. Peterman. He's back, with a film crew and equipment."

"Why?"

"He says he wants to make a documentary about the castle and what's been going on."

"The bloody hell he will."

He stepped through the door to see the crew unloading huge black steamer trunks, dozens of lengths of pipe, lights, sound equipment, and other paraphernalia associated with moviemaking.

"Hi, Inspector," Peterman said. "Thought you'd never see me again?"

I waited for George to substitute "hope" for "thought." He didn't. Instead, he said, "Move that truck."

"Why?"

"Don't ask me why, Mr. Peterman. Just pack your stuff and leave."

"Now, wait a minute," Peterman said. "I'm a paying guest here."

"Yes, *you* are. But *they* aren't."

"They're staying in that other hotel down the road. All I need is a place for the equipment. We'll keep out of your way, shoot most of it outdoors. Mrs. Fletcher, here, is going to be our first interview."

"Mr. Peterman, I'm sure you are, at heart, a very nice person, but—"

"George," I said, "maybe it won't be so bad. At least hear him out."

"Right," Peterman said. "Hear me out."

"You've agreed to be interviewed?" George asked me.

"No. But that doesn't matter. Come inside." I said to Peterman, "Why don't you leave the equipment in the truck and park it behind those outbuildings. I'm sure it will be safe there."

The three-man crew looked to Peterman for instructions. He looked to me. I nodded. "Okay," he said. "You guys load it back up and move the truck over there. Walk down to your hotel and get some dinner. I'll call you first thing in the morning. Be ready to go at seven."

I turned to say something to George, but he'd already left the steps and returned to his office. I suggested to Peterman that he stay out of George's way until I'd had a chance to speak with him.

"You're going to help me get through to him?" he asked.

"Yes."

"How come?"

"I may want a favor from you."

He smiled. "Okay. You rub my back, I rub yours."

"I'd prefer another analogy," I said. "I'll see you at dinner."

I went to my room to get ready for what had

been billed as a "special dinner." After I'd freshened up in the pretty bathroom, and was changing clothes, my attention was drawn to the small mural stair leading to the tiny, low-ceilinged room I'd peeked into upon arriving. I tried to visualize its location in relationship to the long hallway outside the room. As I recalled, there was a door in the hallway that could lead to it. I stepped into the hall and went to the door, tried the handle. Locked. Either it led to another set of steps to that room, or was a closet of some sort.

I returned to my room and slowly went up the mural stair. The room looked, of course, exactly as it had when I first peered into it. But that time, I'd only glanced about, and was there for no more than a few seconds.

There wasn't much to see. It was dark because there were no windows, and the space appeared to be empty. A storage area, I surmised.

But as my eyes acclimated to the gloom, I noticed a small, vague shape in one corner. Hunched over, I went to it, got down on my knees, and touched it. It was a portable tape recorder. I checked for an electrical cord. There was none; it must have been battery powered.

The bigger question, of course, was why would there be a tape recorder in that particular room?

I returned to my room and from my purse took a tiny penlight flashlight I always carry when traveling in the event of hotel power failures. I went up the stairs again, trained the beam on the recorder, and pushed "PLAY."

"*Gie a heize*," an ethereal, breathy woman's voice said through the speakers.

The lady in white.

I pressed "REWIND" and listened again.

And again.

And then one final time.

The special dinner that night was "Cullen Skink," which George explained was a Scottish fish stew, usually based upon the use of haddock, and dating back centuries. "Skink" was an old Scottish word for stew; Cullen referred to the fishing village of Cullen, on the Moray Firth, where the stew was first introduced.

Charlene Sassi, our cooking expert, told us gleefully that Mrs. Gower allowed her to be in the kitchen to observe the preparation of the evening's fare. "She uses lots of bay leaf and leek, and has a heavy hand with the salt and pepper."

"Not good for my blood pressure," Seth said.

"Or your figure, either," Charlene said. "Not with all the butter she uses."

We were a full table again. Everyone from the Cabot Cove contingent was there, along with Dr. and Mrs. Symington, and the Petermans. Naturally, talk turned to Fiona and her disappearance.

As the others discussed it, George leaned to me and said, "I forgot to mention that Constable McKay had the cross from the bridge analyzed."

"I thought he had to send it away," I said.

"He can do basic blood testing. It was human blood."

"No doubt about it?"

"Not according to him."

"What about Fiona's shoes?"

"He hasn't gotten around to that yet, said he'd try to get it done in the morning if he can steal some of Doc Lord's time. Lord is Wick's coroner, among other things. He did the test on the cross."

"Why didn't you call him when Seth was sick?"

"Lord is a vet."

"Oh."

Despite its salty flavor, the fish stew was excellent, and filling. Apple pie with ice cream (how American), and coffee topped off the meal, sending us to the drawing room pounds heavier.

"Mrs. Fletcher," Dr. Symington said. "Please, a few minutes of your time."

"All right."

We moved to a corner of the room. "What can I do for you?" I asked.

"Answer a question for me."

"Of course."

"You said you saw the castle's lady in white the first night you were here."

"That's right."

"Had you been told about her by anyone prior to your sighting?"

"Let me think. Yes. George Sutherland told me about her earlier that evening. He said she was a descendant of the famous Scottish witch, Isabell Gowdie."

"Yes. I am familiar with that history. But something strikes me as quite strange about your sighting, Mrs. Fletcher."

"Which is?"

"I believe you said the lady in white *spoke* to you."

I laughed. "I thought I heard a few words. But looking back on the incident, I'm convinced I didn't."

"Are you quite certain?"

"No. That's the point. I probably never even saw her, let alone heard her speak."

"It pleases me to hear that."

"Why?"

"Sightings of spiritual beings are never accompanied by spoken words."

"Never?"

"Never. You see, Mrs. Fletcher, the prevailing school of thought among my fellow researchers is that when a spirit returns after having died a violent death, as Evelyn Gowdie did, its voice is deliberately muted by the mystical powers that allow it to return. This is especially true when someone is killed because of having practiced witchcraft. The cross on the throat is not incidental. It assures that the witch will no longer be capable of verbally spreading her evil curses."

"Let me ask you something, Doctor."

"Yes?"

"What if I *did* hear the lady in white say something? What would you and your colleagues say to that? How would you explain it?"

"Hmmm. I would have to confer with them, were that the case. Of course, Mrs. Fletcher, sightings of so-called ghosts and spirits do not have verification in the scientific community. Have you noticed the unusual light patterns of the castle?"

"Yes I have. The overall light in this entire area of northern Scotland is different. Because we're so far north?"

"That, and the tendency of the sky to combine varying and conflicting phenomena."

"I've noticed that, too."

"The light conditions your first night here at Sutherland Castle—the night you think you saw the alleged lady in white—are very much like they are tonight."

"Really?"

"Yes. I've been charting it on an hourly basis."

"I didn't realize that."

"I wouldn't be surprised if you saw her again this evening."

"I certainly hope you're wrong."

"I don't think I am, Mrs. Fletcher. It will be interesting to see whether my prediction proves to be correct. You will, of course, immediately report any sighting to me."

"I promise I will—*if* I see the lady again. I'd better get back to my friends, Doctor. Thank you for sharing your thoughts with me."

"All in the interest of science, Mrs. Fletcher. You are a very special person."

"How so?"

"Because you are a writer. Writers possess a certain sensitivity. The chances of you seeing spirits is enhanced. And, you are a woman."

"What about *male* writers?"

"Better than male bricklayers." He giggled at his observation. "But the female has a built-in greater receptivity to such suggestion. Enjoy your friends, Mrs. Fletcher. And keep your eyes open."

I joined Mort and Maureen Metzger, Seth Hazlitt, and others, who were being served after-dinner drinks by Forbes and Malcolm James.

"What was the good doctor talking to you about?" Seth asked.

"Ghosts."

"The man's a weirdo," Mort said. "Must have escaped from some Scottish nuthouse."

"Actually, he's very nice," I said. "He says I might see the lady in white again tonight."

"Silliness," Seth said.

"Spoken like a man," I said. "Dr. Symington says women have greater sensitivity for seeing spirits than men."

"That's because women believe everything they hear and see," said Mort.

"That's not true," Maureen said. "You're such a male chauvinist."

"Just speakin' the truth. Right, Seth?"

"Not an argument I wish to pursue," Seth said.

George Sutherland joined us. "What's the entertainment tonight?" he asked.

"Charades?" Maureen said eagerly.

"I don't like that game," Mort said.

"Because you're not too good at it," Seth said.

"I was as good as you."

"No you aren't. I'd like to play."

"I'll see if I can interest the others," Maureen said. "You'll play, won't you, Jess?"

"Not tonight," I answered.

"Not feeling well?" she asked.

"Feeling fine," I said. "But Dr. Symington's belief that I might see the lady in white again tonight intrigues me. I thought I'd conduct a little experiment."

"Oh?" Seth said. "What sort a' experiment?"

"Make myself available to her. Help the process along."

My friends looked at each other quizzically.

I laughed. "Wouldn't it be interesting if I actually could *will* her to appear for me?"

"Something to drink, Mrs. Fletcher?" Malcolm asked.

"Does alcohol enhance the ability to see spirits?" I asked the group.

"Not likely," Seth said. "When do you intend to conduct this so-called experiment, Jessica?"

"Oh, I don't know. In an hour. You're free to join me."

"The lady in white might not like a crowd," Robert Walters said.

"I'll take that chance," I said. "Besides, there should be witnesses to any experiment. Maybe you'll see her, too."

Malcolm was still waiting for my answer. "A soft drink," I said. "Lemonade?"

"*Ay*, ma'am. We have that."

After he delivered my drink, George and I walked out into the courtyard.

"Lovely night," he said.

"Exquisite."

"So you're going through with your plan?"

"Yes."

"I'm afraid I still don't grasp the significance of the things you mentioned."

"I'm not sure I do, either, George. But if I'm right in my supposition, these disparate things support it. It's worth a try."

"Peterman has agreed?"

"Yes. He's really not a bad sort. He's just—well, he's just Hollywood."

"Remind me to not vacation there. In *Hollywood*."

I laughed and touched his arm. "I'll remind you at regular intervals. Can I make that call now?"

"Of course. I left Lord's number on my desk."

"Thanks, George. If it works, this nightmare you've been living might be over."

"If it is, Jessica Fletcher, I'll be in your eternal debt." He smiled. "A situation I would not find unpleasant."

"Are you playing charades?"

"No. But I'll watch until it's time for your ghost-sighting adventure."

"I'll join you."

Everyone had gathered in the living room, and sides had been chosen.

"Where's the Hollywood couple?" Mort asked. "They don't want to play?"

"No great loss," Seth said.

Dr. Symington appeared at the door.

"Want to play charades, Doc?" Mort asked.

Symington shook his head, motioned for me to join him outside the room.

"I understand you intend to see her," he said.

"Yes. You inspired me."

"I would like to observe."

"By all means. I've invited my friends to watch, too."

"Not wise, Mrs. Fletcher. It might frighten her."

"Maybe they can stand with you out of sight."

"If you insist. When will you try?"

"In an hour."

"I will be there."

George and I passed the hour watching a spirited game of charades. Seth's challenge of Mort had inspired our sheriff. He played with surprising enthusiasm, and even skill on occasion.

As though someone had planned a cue, the hour ended with Charlene's team acting out the motion picture *The Ghost and Mrs. Muir*. Seth guessed it, to applause from his teammates.

Dr. Symington came up behind me. "It is time, Mrs. Fletcher," he said in his pinched, high voice.

"Yes. I think it is," I said.

Everyone looked at me as I stood. "Ready?" I asked.

They followed me from the room to the wide staircase leading upstairs. I paused, turned, and said, "Wish me luck."

We ascended the stairs and gathered in the hallway.

"This where you saw her?" Mort asked.

"Yes," I said. "I suggest everyone back off to over there." I pointed to a spot a dozen feet away, and they moved to it, joining Dr. Symington, who stood holding a notebook.

"How do you intend to summon her?" George asked.

"I have no idea," I said. "Maybe I'll just ask her to appear. Lady in White. Are you there?"

"See her?" Mort asked.

"Quiet," Dr. Symington said sternly.

"Hello?" I said, speaking louder this time. "It's me, Jessica Fletcher. We met a few evenings ago."

I turned, looked at my witnesses, and shrugged.

"Maybe you should offer her food," Mort said. "Like leavin' somethin' for Santa Claus."

"Please, be quiet," Symington said.

"Hey, don't tell me to shut up," Mort said.

I looked at Mort and put my index finger to my lips.

"Seems to me this is all a—"

I interrupted Seth by saying, "I'm your friend, Lady in White. I just want to say hello."

There was total silence until Susan Shevlin whispered, "Try again, Jess."

"Lady in White," I said. "If you can hear me, I'd really like to—"

We were all distracted by sounds from outside the castle. I looked at George, whose expression said he was concerned. He held up his finger to indicate we should continue what we were doing, and went downstairs. The sounds grew louder; it sounded like a large group of people.

"Lady in White, if you can hear me, I—"

"Can you see her?" Dr. Symington asked.

"*Yes!*" I shouted. "I see her. Hello. Thank you for coming."

The volume outside had now reached fever pitch. People were chanting—"*Close the castle! Sutherland must go! Close the castle! Sutherland must go!*" Flickering orange light from torches could be seen through the windows.

"What is she wearing?" Dr. Symington asked, coming to my side.

"She's wearing—"

"*Gie a heize.*"

"What?" I said. "Would you repeat that?"

But I knew it wouldn't be repeated, and turned my attention to the commotion outside.

"What's goin' on out there?" Seth asked.

"Let's go see," Mort said.

"No, wait," I said.

"For what?" Jim Shevlin asked.

"For Mr. Peterman to confirm he got it all."

"What are you talking about?" Seth asked.

"Mr. Peterman, come out."

Everyone watched as the flamboyant producer of horror films, accompanied by his cameraman carrying a portable camcorder, emerged from a door directly across the hall from where I'd stood. They'd been hidden from view of the others.

"Did you get it?" I asked.

"Sure did," Peterman said. "Got it all."

Dr. Symington sounded incredulous: "You put the Lady in White on film?"

I answered: "No. But he has on film who's behind what's been going on here."

"Wait a minute," Mort said, joining us. "I don't get it. What are you saying, Mrs. F.?"

"I suggest we go downstairs and see what's going on outside. Once that's settled, we can gather in the living room and watch Mr. Peterman's video. I think you'll all find it v-e-r-y interesting."

Chapter Twenty

We all went to the castle's front door, where George had confronted dozens of townspeople, some carrying torches, others weapons. Evan Lochbuie was at the head of the crowd, leading the chant: *"Close the castle! Sutherland must go! Close the castle! Sutherland must go!"*

Constable McKay, and his deputy, Bob, stood to one side. I recognized Daisy Wemyss's uncle, owner of the sporting goods shop, and the big man who'd threatened George in the Birks of Aberfeldy.

"Go home," George shouted. "Don't be fools. Go home to your families."

"Not until you've gone home for good," someone yelled. "To bloody London."

George looked to McKay, who seemed disinterested in what was going on. "You'd better take charge, Horace," he said.

"And I told you, George, it was out of my

hands. Too much water under the bridge. Too much evil."

I stepped to George's side.

"Go back inside," he said to me.

"Not on your life," I said. "This reminds me of *The Hunchback of Notre Dame*."

My comment caused him to smile. But only for a second.

Like what happened in London at the Tower of London, my next move was involuntary. I stepped in front of George, held up my hands, and said in as loud a voice as I could muster, "You are all mistaken. There is no evil at Sutherland Castle. No ghosts. No witchcraft."

"It's Sutherland's bloody lassie," a man said. "Pay no heed to her."

"Listen to me," I said, straining my vocal cords. "If you'll put out your torches, and put down your weapons, I can prove it to you." I turned and asked George, "Can I invite them in?"

"Invite them in? I think that would be—"

"Please, George. At least let me try."

"All right."

"Put down your weapons and extinguish your torches," I said. "Then come inside. I'll show you what I'm talking about."

There was a lot of muttering as they decided whether to accept my invitation. I looked directly at Constable McKay, who seemed especially confused. I said to him, "Take charge, Constable. Tell them to do what I said."

George reinforced my message: "Listen to her, Horace. If you don't, you'll have bloodshed on your hands."

McKay looked to the others, held up his hands, and said, "Nothing to be lost hearing what she has to say," he shouted. To me: "Just a few minutes, Mrs. Fletcher. No more. You can say your piece."

"Fair enough," I said.

They followed us into the castle and to the living room, where the others had congregated. Even in the large space, the crowd spilled into the hallway. I was pleased to see that Brock Peterman had already set up a video screen in one corner.

"Where's Malcolm?" I asked Forbes, who stood ready to serve refreshments should George ask him to do that. But drinks weren't on anyone's mind at the moment.

"In the kitchen with Mrs. Gower," he replied in his low, measured, flat voice.

"Please get him and Mrs. Gower for me," I said.

Forbes looked to George. "Go on," George said. "Do what Mrs. Fletcher has asked."

While waiting for them, I went to where Peterman stood next to his video equipment. "All set?" I asked.

"Yup. I took a look while you were outside.

Pretty clear, considering the lack of light. The lens I used is a monster. Picks up images in damn near-total darkness."

"Good," I said.

Malcolm came into the room, followed by the glowering Mrs. Gower. He came to me. "Mrs. Fletcher," he said, "I can't be staying. My mum's come down sick and—"

"It will only take a moment, Malcolm. I promise you that. Just a minute."

"Sorry, ma'am, but—"

"You stay put," George said to him, placing his large hand on the young man's shoulder.

I turned to Ken Sassi. "Ken, would you please get me that chair?"

He pulled over a sturdy, broad wooden chair with a flat seat and held my hand as I stepped up onto it. I raised my hands; the conversations slowly dwindled, leaving me with the floor, as it were.

"May I have your attention?" I said to the few people still talking. They fell silent. "Thank you. And thank you for allowing me these few minutes to explain what's been going on here at Sutherland Castle, and in your lovely village of Wick."

I paused to gain a sense of how they were receiving me. So far, so good. I had their attention.

I continued: "You've come here tonight because you're afraid."

"I not be afraid," a man said. "I fear nothing and no one."

"I'm sure you're very brave," I said. "You all are. You've proved that over many years of strife and hard times. But you have wives and children. You want the best for them, just as you want the best for your beloved Wick."

"Is there something wrong with that?" another man asked.

"No. And that is exactly my point. The strange things that have been occurring here, and in the village, have set everyone on edge, which is perfectly understandable. The problem is that none of it is the result of some evil force being cast upon you by this castle or its owner, George Sutherland."

"Young Daisy Wemyss was killed like she was a witch," her uncle, the shopkeeper, said. "A dear and loving niece, she was. Killed with the pitchfork through her heart, and a cross carved on her young throat. What do you say to that?"

"I say her murder was a terrible tragedy, one that never should have happened. But it was not witchcraft or evil spirits that killed Daisy Wemyss. It was not Sutherland Castle. It was not some bizarre link to the past, to the way Evelyn Gowdie was killed twenty years ago, or Isabell Gowdie more than three hundred years before that. Daisy Wemyss was killed because—"

I saw Malcolm edging away from the crowd in the direction of a door. "Malcolm," I said loudly. "Don't leave."

"What's he got to do with any of this?" someone asked.

"I'll show you," I said. "Mr. Peterman, would you do the honors."

"Somebody lower the lights," Peterman said. George obliged him.

"Go ahead," I said to Peterman.

He started the videotape. A series of patterns filled the screen, multicolored stripes, a series of numbers, and then a murky, shadowy scene.

"Watch closely," I said.

Everyone squeezed close together in order to see the screen. Some couldn't; "What's it say?" they asked others who had a clear view.

The scene taking shape on the screen was of the upstairs hallway, videotaped from the secluded vantage point of the room across from the door that I surmised led to the low-ceilinged, empty room up the stairs from my room—the room in which I'd discovered the battery-powered tape recorder.

The room was deathly still.

The tape rolled on.

And my voice came through the speakers.

"I suggest everyone back off to over there."

George's voice: *"How do you intend to summon her?"*

I replied, *"I have no idea. Maybe I'll just ask her to appear. Lady in White. Are you there?"*

"See her?" Mort asked.

"Quiet." It was Dr. Symington's voice.

"Hello?" I said, louder this time. *"It's me, Jessica Fletcher. We met a few evenings ago."*

Mort Metzger: *"Maybe you should offer her food. Like leavin' somethin' for Santa Claus."*

Dr. Symington: *"Please, be quiet."*

Mort Metzger: *"Hey, don't tell me to shut up."*

Seth Hazlitt: *"Seems to me this is all a—"*

I interrupted him. *"I'm your friend, Lady in White. I just want to say hello."*

Susan Shevlin's whisper could be heard: *"Try again, Jess."*

I did. *"Lady in White. If you can hear me, I'd really like to—"*

Faint sounds from outside the castle intruded on the sound track.

I said, *"Lady in White, if you can hear me, I—"*

Dr. Symington: *"Can you see her?"*

"Yes!" I shouted. *"I see her. Hello. Thank you for coming."*

Now the chants from outside could be heard: *"Close the castle! Sutherland must go! Close the castle! Sutherland must go!"* The visual included faint orange flickering from their torches.

"What is she wearing?" Dr. Symington asked.

"She's wearing—"

"Gie a heize."

"What?" I said. *"Would you repeat that?"*

"What's goin' on out there?" Seth asked, referring to the noise from outside.

Mort Metzger: *"Let's go see."*

"No, wait," I said.

"For what?" Jim Shevlin asked.

"For Mr. Peterman to confirm he got it all," I said.

Seth Hazlitt: *"What are you talking about?"*

I replied, *"Mr. Peterman, come out. Did you get it?"*

"Sure did," Peterman said. *"Got it all."*

Dr. Symington: *"You put the lady in white on film?"*

"No," I replied. *"But he has on film who's behind what's been going on here."*

Mort Metzger: *"Wait a minute. I don't get it. What are you saying, Mrs. F.?"*

"I suggest we go downstairs and see what's going on outside. Once that's settled, we can gather in the living room and watch Mr. Peterman's video. I think you'll all find it v-e-r-y interesting."

Peterman stopped the VCR; George turned up the lights.

"What's this all mean?" Constable McKay asked, hands on hips, chin in a defiant set.

"Did you *really* see the lady in white?" Charlene Sassi asked.

"I'll get to that in a moment," I said. "In the meantime, there's some more video to watch."

George dimmed the lights again, and Peterman rolled the video from where he'd left off.

We'd all left the upstairs landing and gone downstairs to see what the ruckus outside the castle was about. Now a second camera was trained on the door in the hallway from its hidden vantage point. We waited for something to happen. It took less than a minute. The door to the hallway opened, and Malcolm James was seen. He poked his head out, looked left and right, stepped from the doorway, closed the door behind him, locked it, and moved quickly out of frame.

"Don't let Malcolm James leave," I said directly to Constable McKay. McKay seemed unsure of what to do. But when Malcolm made another attempt to depart, the constable restrained him.

"You've got your nerve," Malcolm said to McKay.

"And you shut up," McKay replied, twisting Malcolm's arm behind him.

"I still don't get it, Jess," Mort Metzger said. "So we saw him coming through a door. What's that mean?"

"It means this," I said. I'd dispatched Jim Shevlin to my room once we'd come downstairs, and had him go up the mural stair to the cramped room in which I'd discovered the recorder. Now Jim handed the recorder to me. I rewound the tape, asked for everyone's attention, and pushed "PLAY."

"Gie a heize."

George looked at me. "What the lady in white said to you," he said.

"Yes. And what Malcolm said one day. Remember?"

"Yes. I remember."

"Listen again," I said.

"Gie a heize."

"Anyone recognize that voice?" I asked.

Puzzled expressions all around—except for Mrs. Gower. The stout, stern cook said, "That would be Fiona."

"That's right, Mrs. Gower," I said. "It's Fiona's voice, recorded by—"

I looked directly at Malcolm, still in Constable McKay's grasp. "Recorded by *you*, Malcolm."

He said nothing in response, but his face and eyes shouted what he was thinking: He wanted to run, to hide, to evaporate.

Ken Sassi helped me down from the chair. I went to Malcolm, raised my eyebrows into question marks, and verbally asked, "Where is Fiona?"

"What are you talking about?" he managed weakly.

"She isn't dead, is she? And you know where she is because you arranged for her to go there."

"Mrs. Fletcher, I swear—"

"I think we've heard enough," the constable said. "I'll take him to the *nick*."

"The what?" Mort Metzger said.

"Jail," George translated.

McKay started to push Malcolm through the crowd, but I stopped him with, "I think you'd better answer a few questions, Constable McKay, before you haul him away."

The constable slowly turned and fixed me in a hard, hateful glare.

"Why did you lie about the blood found on the bridge, and on Fiona's shoes?"

"You're calling me a liar, are you?" he said.

"Yes. I called Dr. Lord, the veterinarian, who tested the blood on both. You said it was human blood. But Dr. Lord told me it was animal blood. Why, Constable McKay, did you deliberately misrepresent his findings?"

I answered for him. "Because you wanted to perpetuate fear in the hearts of Wick's citizens."

McKay again started to push through the crowd. This time, George stepped in his way. "I think you ought to hear Mrs. Fletcher out," he said. "In fact, as a ranking law enforcement officer, I insist that you do."

Mort Metzger joined George, saying, "And I'm

here to assist as duly elected sheriff of Cabot Cove, Maine, U.S.A."

"Stand aside," McKay said. "Don't be breaking *my* law."

"*Your* law," I said. "That's exactly it. You took the law into your own hands to serve the interests of others. How much did the London investors promise to pay you, Constable McKay? How much money bought your cooperation in creating an atmosphere of fear in order to force Inspector Sutherland to sell his family's homestead?"

McKay stood tall and mute. I turned to Malcolm.

"Was having your novel published that important to you, Malcolm, that you went along with this scheme?"

"They told me that—"

"Shut up," McKay said.

"You go right ahead and keep talking, Malcolm," I said. "If you don't explain yourself, you'll end up spending the rest of your life behind bars for the murder of Daisy Wemyss."

His voice came from high in his throat. He fought back tears as he said, "Oh, no, Mrs. Fletcher. I had nothing to do with that. Not with poor Daisy. All I did was—"

McKay's hand went to Malcolm's throat, but George's move was fast and sure. He shoved McKay against a wall, his own hand at the constable's throat. Mort jumped in, helping to keep McKay in place.

Malcolm was now free. But instead of running, he started babbling: "I did nothing to harm anyone," he said, his voice still high and shaky. "They told me if I'd set up the recorder and scare guests at the castle, they'd have my book published."

"By Flemming House, a subsidy publisher," I said. "They paid that publisher to publish your novel. I happen to know something about Flemming House because my publisher in London bought the company. They'll publish anyone's book, Malcolm, good or bad, for enough money."

"They told me they had connections," Malcolm said. "They told me Flemming House loved my book and thought it would be a best-seller all over the world."

"They lied to you," I said. "Now, where is Fiona? She isn't dead, is she?"

He sadly shook his head.

"Where is she?"

"John o' Groat's. With a girlfriend. I sent her there. That's what he told me to do."

"Who told you to send her there?"

Malcolm looked to where George and Mort still restrained Constable McKay.

"Constable McKay?" I asked.

Malcolm shook his head. "No. Him."

He pointed across the room to Evan Lochbuie, who stood apart from the crowd.

"Mr. Lochbuie?" I said.

"He's the one. Told me Constable McKay got the word from the investors to get her away from Wick. He gave me money and sent a car to drive her."

"And told you to leave her dress and shoes here so animal blood could be smeared on them to make it seem another murder had taken place."

"That's right. They told me to do everything, Mrs. Fletcher. But I never wanted no one killed. Not Daisy, for sure. Not anyone."

I turned to say something to Lochbuie, but he was gone. George saw the dismay on my face and said, "Don't worry, Jessica. I'll see that he's picked up, along with everyone else involved in this vile scheme."

"Count on me, too, George," Mort said. "Hey, we make a good team."

Chapter Twenty-one

"I believe I'll try one of these Sheep Dips," Mort Metzger said, pointing to it on the menu of single-malt scotches in the Athenaeum's Whisky Bar.

"Sheep Dip?" Seth Hazlitt said, his face mirroring his disgust. "You know what that is."

"It's also a very fine whiskey," the waiter said. "A vatted malt." He looked to me next. "And you, ma'am?"

"Club soda," I said.

"Come on, Jess," Charlene Sassi said. "You deserve a stiff drink after what you've been through."

"Couldn't possibly," I said. "I'd fall on my nose, I'm afraid. But you enjoy yourself. We only have this last night in London."

My other friends from Cabot Cove ordered drinks, and we settled in for an hour of celebratory conversation. The mysteries of Sutherland Castle had been revealed for what they were—a scam to persuade George Sutherland to sell the castle to the London investors. Constable McKay and his cabal admitted to Scotland Yard inspectors called in by George that they'd conspired to force George to sell. Even our gillie, Rufus Innes, had been involved, leading us to that spot in the river by the bridge, where the big man who'd tried to pick a fight with George in the pub waited to toss the log at me, not to try and kill me, he claimed, but only to instill additional fear. I tended to believe him.

If it had only ended up a clumsy scam, that would have been bad enough. But they went too far—much too far—when they decided that a *real* murder had to take place to push the townspeople over the edge. Daisy Wemyss was sacrificed to that end. No one admitted to having murdered her, but George was told that evidence pointed to Evan Lochbuie, the town "nut," who turned out to not be so crazy after all. Evil? Yes. Warped? Absolutely. A murderer? That would be determined at trial.

The fate of Malcolm and Fiona was unclear. The girl obviously had been used, and shouldn't face criminal charges, unless an overzealous prosecutor decided to include her in the conspiracy charge.

As for Malcolm, he'd gotten in a lot deeper, although murder wouldn't be one of the charges against him. But he'd taken money to advance the plot, and that would be enough to indict him.

Those who gave him the money to conspire in the plot, the London investors, were also facing criminal indictment.

Funny, how we can misread people. I'd thought all along that Forbes, the dour jack-of-all-trades in George's employ, was involved. It turned out he's only that, a sour, sullen individual who was absent when they handed out personality genes.

Everyone was served their single-malt scotches, and Seth proposed a toast: "To one of the more interesting vacations of my life."

"That's appropriately noncommittal," Jim Shevlin said. "But I'll drink to it."

Rims clinked all the way around.

"Jessica," Seth said, "there's still that large question looming."

"Which one is that, Seth?"

"The lady in white. You said you saw her. Twice. Now I understand about the voice, and the tape recorder. Meant to deceive. But you said you *saw* her. What did they do to create a visual of her in the hallway?"

"Nothing, except to use the power of suggestion. Tell me not to think of purple elephants and that's all I'll think of. George had told me, in detail, about the supposed lady in white who haunted the castle. I was primed to see her, especially because the light characteristics in northern Scotland are conducive to creating imaginary images at certain times. I *thought* I'd seen her the first night we were there. But I deliberately said I'd seen her the second time to prompt Malcolm to use the tape recorder. It worked. He did."

"Well, all I can say is that you saved a castle," Pete Walters said. "Your friend, George, must be grateful."

"Yes, he is, although he isn't sure he'll keep the place. I hope he does. It means so much to him."

"That Brock Peterman turned out okay," pilot Jed Richardson said. "Doesn't make me like him any better, but he did help you out."

"For his own purposes," I said. "He's going ahead with his documentary, only now he has a real ending for it. Poor Malcolm. He was waiting for an ending, too. A shame he ended up part of it."

"What about Dr. Symington?" Susan Shevlin asked. "A strange bird."

"And helpful. When he told me ghosts never speak when sighted, it put the icing on the cake for me. That's when I decided to attempt to set things up the way I did."

The waiter returned and asked if we wanted another round of drinks. Everyone ordered different single-malt scotches from the menu, which boasted such names as Bunnahabhain, Royal Brackla, Miltonduff, and Tullibardine.

"Hate to leave in the mornin'," Seth said, leading the second toast of the evening. "What time's the bus departing for the airport?"

"Nine," I said. "I won't be on it. I'm meeting George for breakfast. He'll drive me to Heathrow."

There were raised eyebrows, and good-natured kidding.

I got up and straightened my skirt. "Have to run," I said.

"Dinner with the dashing inspector?" Seth asked.

"No. Dinner with my publisher, Archie Semple. An interview with a magazine. Then to bed. This lady is very tired."

"See you at the airport, Mrs. F.," Mort said.

"Yes, you will."

"Hey, Mrs. F., what did you think of George putting me in for a special commendation from Scotland Yard?"

"I think it was a very nice thing to do, Mort. And much deserved."

He beamed. "He'll be sending me a plaque. Thought I'd hang it out front of the station house. You know, where people can see it when they come in."

I was about to leave when the Athenaeum's executive manager and my friend, Sally Bulloch, bounded into the room.

"Just leaving?" she asked.

"Yes," I said.

"Catch you for breakfast before you leave?"

"I'd love to, Sally, but I have a breakfast—appointment."

"Another time, then. I have to talk to you. I just had an incredible experience that would make a marvelous basis for your next book."

"Oh?"

"One of our guests—a regular one, very rich and famous—just told me that when he was walking down the hall to his room last night, he saw—" She giggled. "He claims he saw a *ghost*."

We stared at her with mouths slightly open.

"Was she wearing white?" I asked.

"Wearing white? *She*? I don't think he indicated a gender."

"Probably just the lighting conditions," I offered. "If he'd been thinking of purple elephants, it wouldn't have happened."

"What?"

"He'd have seen purple elephants instead. Have to run. You and your hotel are always a delight." We hugged. "Take care of my friends tonight. I have a feeling they're going for the free bottle."

"I hate to see you go," George said as we drove to the airport the following morning.

"And I hate to go," I said.

"I've decided to keep Sutherland Castle."

"I'm not surprised. It's a lovely place. I'm sure with the right people running it as a hotel, it will do very nicely."

"And I should be able to find the right people, now that everyone in Wick isn't afraid to work there. I've put Mrs. Gower in charge. She's rising to the occasion; told me it was about time I recognized her talents beyond the kitchen. And Forbes will stay. Maybe I'll pay for him to take a Dale Carnegie course."

"Sounds like everything's falling in place," I said.

"Not everything."

"What's missing?"

"You. I want you to return to Wick, Jessica. I want you to come back alone so we can spend truly productive time together. We barely had time to talk, with all that went on this past week."

"But it ended up on a positive note. I loved the Highland Games, although I must admit I was a little worried when that giant of a man came running in our direction, carrying that huge tree trunk."

"Carrying the *caber*, he was. Afraid he'd toss it at you?"

"It crossed my mind."

"He threw it quite far. Throwing the caber is the highlight of the games."

"An impressive display of strength and balance.

George, about my coming back. You know I will. I have a book to write. After I'm done, we'll plan to get together again. That's the best I can offer."

"*Ay*. It will have to do. I'll take what I can get of Jessica Fletcher."

"I'll come in and wait with you," he said as we pulled up in front of the British Airways Terminal at Heathrow Airport.

"Please don't," I said. "It's easier saying good-bye here. My friends will be waiting for me. Understand?"

"Of course."

There was that awkward moment of silence when two people who like each other very much search for final words of parting. George finally said, "I won't put you in an awkward position, Jessica. Go on. Get out. The porter there will take your bags. We'll be in touch."

He said it without looking at me.

"George."

He faced me. "Yes?"

"Thank you for being you."

My lips brushed his, and I squeezed his hand. "Until next time," I said.

"*Ay*. I pray it comes fast. Safe home."

"Yes. Safe home."

"Will you be giving us a concert?" the pretty and pert British Airways flight attendant asked as she helped stow my bagpipes in a closet aboard the 747.

"Not unless you want to start a revolt by your other passengers," I said.

Her laugh was like a bell. "No, we can't have that, can we?" she said in a Scottish brogue.

The flight was smooth, the service caring, and we landed on time at New York's Kennedy Airport. We took our connecting flight to Bangor, and a hired minibus to Cabot Cove.

"Good to be home," Seth said, stretching as he climbed out of the bus.

"It always is," I said.

"You don't look too sure about that," he said.

"Oh, I'm sure about it," I said.

"Ready to start your next book?"

"No. I need some time for myself before getting involved with any new fictitious characters. I thought I'd take a few lessons."

"In what?"

"In playing the pipes."

"Nobody in Cabot Cove plays 'em, let alone teach 'em," he said.

"Then, I'll just have to become self-taught."

"Knowin' you, Jessica, you'll become the best bagpipes player in Maine."

"The *only* bagpipes player in Maine."

"You'll be missing him, won't you?"

"Who? George? Yes, of course."

"See you for breakfast at Mara's?"

"That sounds fine. See you then."

I closed the door to my house, stood in the living room, and looked at my bagpipes. A swell of nostalgia swept over me, and my eyes misted. I thought of something George Sutherland had said to me when we last parted. It was in San Francisco, where I'd been promoting my latest novel, and he'd attended an international police conference. We'd ended up solving a murder and helping a falsely accused woman clear herself. He'd paraphrased the famed Scottish poet, Robert Burns:

"My Jessica's asleep by the murmuring stream; Flow gently sweet Afton, disturb not her dream."

Recalling his words made me smile.

I made a cup of tea, sat in my living room with the pipes on my lap, placed the blowpipe in my mouth, and blew hard.

It was music to my ears.

Join Jessica on the
QE2!

Sail into another murder in
the next *Murder, She Wrote* mystery:

MURDER ON THE *QE2*
by Jessica Fletcher
and Donald Bain

Available from Signet

The older I become, the harder it is to surprise me.

But when Matt Miller, my agent of many years, called late last winter from New York with a new and unusual project for me, I was surprised to the point of near shock.

"I can't believe this," I said. "Why me?"

"The fact that you're the world's most success-ful and best-known murder mystery writer is rea-son enough, Jess." He laughed. "I've delivered lots of good news to you, but I've never heard you so excited before. As I said, it doesn't pay that much, and it means having to drop the book you're working on for a month, but—"

"Matt," I said, "one day soon I'll explain why I'm so enthusiastic. In the meantime, I'm running late for a lunch date with Seth Hazlitt. You re-member him?"

"Sure. Cabot Cove's resident doc. Say hello for me."

"I certainly will. Can I call you later for more details?"

"I'll be here all day."

I hung up, giggled, and then let out a loud squeal of joy. But the euphoria lasted only a few minutes—until a wave of sadness displaced it.

It was twenty years ago that I made my first, and only transatlantic crossing on the fabled *Queen Elizabeth 2*, the *grande dame* of all ocean liners. My husband, Frank, was alive then, and had given me—us—the crossing as a joint Christmas present. We set sail on May 28th of that year and reveled in the ship's majesty, and the pampering we received from its large international staff.

I remembered that trip as clearly as though I'd taken it yesterday.

Frank and I stood on the *QE2*'s highest deck, arms about each other, peering into the distance at Southampton, England, after five glorious days at sea.

"Know what I think, Jess?" he said.

"No. What?"

"I think we should make this a yearly event. Save toward it all year. Treat ourselves to this grand experience every year we're alive and can enjoy it together."

I hugged him tighter. "For a conservative New

Englander, Frank, you do have your extravagant moments."

He laughed. "Yes, I do," he said. "When it concerns you."

We kissed, and spent the next week in London, extending the moment.

We never sailed on the *QE2* again. Frank became very ill shortly after we returned home, and died later that year. Of course, I often thought about crossing on the *QE2* again, especially each year when May 28th rolls around. But I could never bring myself to simply call Susan Shevlin, my travel agent in Cabot Cove, and book myself a stateroom. I just didn't want to do it without Frank.

But this was different. This was business.

"Say again, Jessica," Dr. Seth Hazlitt said at lunch. We'd been best of friends for more years than I care to admit.

"They want me to lecture about writing murder mysteries on the *QE2* between New York and Southampton. I'll be one of a group of people lecturing on different subjects. And I'm to write a murder mystery play that will be acted by a Los Angeles theatrical troupe."

"Sounds like a fairly good thing," he said in his usual understated way. "How do you feel about travelin' alone?"

"I hadn't thought about it, Seth. I travel alone all the time."

"But, not on a big ship crossin' the Atlantic Ocean."

"What difference does that make?"

"Makes a considerable difference, it seems to me. I could go along with you."

"That would be lovely, Seth, but—"

"We'll talk more about it. In the meantime, finish your lobster roll. Especially good, wouldn't you say?"

"Yes, Seth. It's especially good."

It was during our first full day at sea that the tragedy struck.

The actors and actresses who were to perform my script had gathered in the Grand Lounge on what's called the Upper Deck, below the Boat Deck and Sun Deck. The director, a delightful young woman named Jill Farkas, started by rehearsing the first murder scene, which was to take place approximately ten minutes into the play. In it, one of the actors, portraying an unsavory loan shark, is confronted by his former wife, who demands money she claims he stole from her when they were still together.

I sat in a comfortable chair at one of the many cocktail tables in the opulent lounge and watched with intense interest and pleasure the scene unveiling before me. The actor and actress were talented performers; they did my words proud.

The actor playing the ex-husband verbally abused his wife onstage. He mocked her, said she was stupid and didn't stand a chance of getting money from him.

Her face flared into anger. She berated him for the lowlife that he was, and said she'd never let him get away with the money stolen from her.

"Why don't you just shut up?" he snarled, his face twisted into a nasty smile.

"No," she said, "I'll shut *you* up, Billy."

She pulled the revolver from her shoulder bag and leveled it at his chest.

"What are you, nuts?" he shouted.

"You've abused me for the last time," she said, fighting back tears.

"Gimme the gun, Helen," he said, taking a step closer to her and extending his hand. "Don't be dumb. You're not gonna shoot me. You're not gonna shoot anybody. Look at yourself. You're shaking like a leaf. Hell, you'll end up shooting off your own foot."

His hand moved closer to her.

Even though I'd written the scene, I was caught up in the tension of the moment. I leaned forward and pressed a finger to my lips. That was the end of dialogue between them. The script called for her to pull the trigger—now!

The report from the blank discharged from the revolver resounded throughout the Grand Lounge. It caused me to sit up straight. I watched as the actor went through his death throes—a little too dramatic and strung out for my taste—and fell to the stage. The actress screamed, dropped the weapon and ran into the wings.

I applauded and joined the troupe on the stage. The other actors and actresses, and Jill Farkas, had come from backstage and we all stood over the slain actor. A red stain slowly expanded on his shirtfront.

"Let's not waste the fake blood on rehearsals," Jill said.

We all waited for him to get up.

"Come on, Joe, the scene's over," an actress said.

But Joe didn't get up. Slowly, but surely, it became apparent that he never would. There were now gasps, moans, a few cries of anguish. Some fell to their knees and tried to shake him into life.

"What's going on?" Graham Flemming, the QE2's social director, asked, joining us onstage.

"He's dead," Jill Farkas said.

"He's *dead*?"

"I'm afraid so," I said, placing my fingertips to his neck in search of a pulse. "Someone obviously replaced the blanks in that gun with live ammunition."

Flemming didn't miss a beat. He turned and looked out over the Grand Lounge. A few people, no more than a dozen, had stopped in to watch the rehearsal, but none of them seemed to be aware of what was really going on.

"Get him out of sight," Flemming said. "Quick!"

The actor was dragged into the wings and out of view of anyone except those of us involved with the play.

"Nobody move," Flemming said. "Just stay put."

He picked up a phone, dialed a shipboard number, and said to whoever answered, "We have a death in the Grand Lounge. Backstage. Get down here with a body cart and something to cover it with."

He hung up and said to us, "Please, say nothing to anyone about this until I've had a chance to discuss it with the captain and security."

"Where will you take him?" I asked.

"The morgue."

"You have a morgue on the *QE2*?"

"Yes, ma'am. Holds four. I ask all of you again, keep this quiet, p-l-e-a-s-e! There's nothing to be gained by creating a panic with the other passengers."

"I think he's right," I said to the actors and

actresses. To him: "But you will get back to us right away."

"As soon as I can get the appropriate people together. Thanks for your cooperation."

The dead actor was wheeled away, covered by a sheet that made it look as though it might have been a food cart. We stood together backstage for a few minutes, mostly in silence. Finally, I said, "I think I'll go to my cabin."

"Yeah, me, too," an actor said.

We dispersed, and I headed for my stateroom on the Quarter Deck, one deck below. But as I poised to open my door, I changed my mind and climbed the stairs to the ship's Sun Deck, the top deck where I'd been wrapped in a blanket earlier that morning and served a delicious cup of bouillon.

The weather was foul. The *QE2* was shrouded in fog, and a mist engulfed me. The sea was rough, causing the ship to rise and fall in a steady pattern.

I went to where Frank and I had stood twenty years earlier, wrapped my arms about myself, and felt tears well up.

Was it the death I'd just witnessed that caused me to cry?

Or was it remembering standing here with my beloved husband during our voyage together, one that was as smooth as silk, and certainly hadn't been marred by a shooting death?

Maybe a little of both, I decided.

I knew one thing: My memories of this transatlantic crossing would be markedly different from the previous one.

FROM THE MYSTERY SERIES
MURDER,
SHE WROTE
by Jessica Fletcher & Donald Bain

Based on the Universal television series
Created by Peter S. Fischer, Richard Levinson & William Link

**Available wherever books are sold or at
penguin.com**

S0013

MURDER, SHE WROTE:

A Slaying in Savannah

by Jessica Fletcher & Donald Bain

Based on the Universal television series
Created by Peter S. Fischer,
Richard Levinson & William Link

When her old friend Tillie passes away, Jessica is surprised to find that she has left her a million dollars. But there's a catch: she will receive it only if she can solve the murder of Tillie's fiancé, Wanamaker Jones.

As Jessica settles into Tillie's Savannah mansion, she soon discovers that Wanamaker's spirit haunts the grounds. And that there are those in Savannah who are waiting to cash in on Tillie's demise—and Jessica's failure.

S822

Penguin Group (USA) Online

What will you be reading tomorrow?

Tom Clancy, Patricia Cornwell, W.E.B. Griffin,
Nora Roberts, William Gibson, Catherine Coulter,
Stephen King, Dean Koontz, Ken Follett,
Nick Hornby, Khaled Hosseini, Kathryn Stockett,
Clive Cussler, John Sandford, Terry McMillan,
Sue Monk Kidd, Amy Tan, J. R. Ward,
Laurell K. Hamilton, Charlaine Harris,
Christine Feehan...

You'll find them all at
penguin.com

*Read excerpts and newsletters,
find tour schedules and reading group guides,
and enter contests.*

Subscribe to Penguin Group (USA) newsletters
and get an exclusive inside look
at exciting new titles and the authors you love
long before everyone else does.

PENGUIN GROUP (USA)
us.penguingroup.com

S0151